He Would Let He...
But He Made the Rules.

"Your fair skin and blond hair may well prove an alluring novelty in Mexico, but keep in mind that this is *my* vineyard, and I won't tolerate any disruptive element." His blazing black eyes burned into hers. "You're here to learn winemaking, not to play the enticing amber witch."

His words angered her; she had done nothing to incur such treatment. "Let me go!" she hissed through trembling lips.

"When you can assure me that you and I understand each other, Señorita Gayle, *then* I will let you go." His anger was now matched by his mockery. "Remember, you are now in *my* country, working in *my* vineyards, and everything here will be done exactly as I say it shall be done!"

FRAN WILSON
traces her love of writing to her grandfather, but her love of romance is her own. A published writer of both fiction and nonfiction, she brings her knowledge of music, travel and Americana to these very special stories of people today—in love.

Dear Reader:

Silhouette Romances is an exciting new publishing venture. We will be presenting the very finest writers of contemporary romantic fiction as well as outstanding new talent in this field. It is our hope that our stories, our heroes and our heroines will give you, the reader, all you want from romantic fiction.

Also, *you* play an important part in our future plans for Silhouette Romances. We welcome any suggestions or comments on our books and I invite you to write to us at the address below.

So, enjoy this book and all the wonderful romances from Silhouette. They're for *you*!

Karen Solem
Editor-in-Chief
Silhouette Books
P.O. Box 769
New York, N.Y. 10019

FRAN WILSON
Amber Wine

Silhouette *Romance*

Published by Silhouette Books New York

America's Publisher of Contemporary Romance

Other Silhouette Romances by Fran Wilson

Where Mountains Wait

SILHOUETTE BOOKS, a Simon & Schuster Division of
GULF & WESTERN CORPORATION
1230 Avenue of the Americas, New York, N.Y. 10020

ISBN: 0-671-57138-9

First Silhouette Books printing March, 1982

10 9 8 7 6 5 4 3 2 1

For I would harvest grapes from off the vine,
And touch the lips I love with amber wine.

F.E.W.

To Pamela and Doug

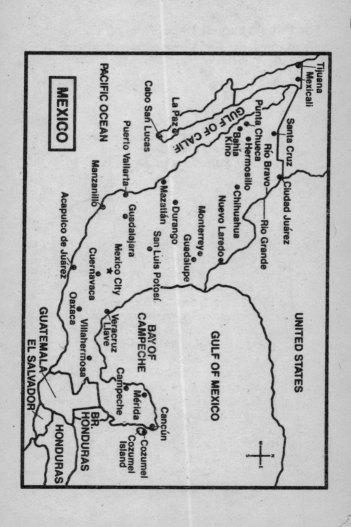

Chapter One

The vista of rolling vineyards stretching as far as the eye could see from either side of the highway startled Gayle into sudden awareness of her surroundings. She had been so absorbed in her turbulent thoughts that she had driven from San Francisco back to the Napa Valley like a well-programmed robot. Without being conscious of her actions, she had kept her foot steadily pressed on the gas pedal, and her hands tensely gripping the wheel had steered the copper sports car up the divided highway toward St. Helena. Letting a sigh of regret pass her lips, she acknowledged to herself that, since leaving the Bay City, she had been thinking of only one thing, and that was the shattering fact that on this sunny day in late August the man she had thought she was going to marry had jilted her.

Her head ached and her eyes felt hot and dry. She edged her sunglasses higher on her small nose. The summer sun had long since burned the early morning fog from the air and now bright rays of afternoon sunlight angled through the windshield directly into her tearless blue eyes. She had not been able to cry earlier, and now she was determined not to. Glancing at the narrow gold watch on her wrist, she saw that it was not yet four o'clock. She wanted to delay going to the house and facing her father. Those discerning gray eyes of his would know at once that something was terribly wrong, and she was not prepared as yet to cope with painful questions.

Wheeling her car sharply, the tires sprayed loose gravel as she drove in past the green and white sign which spelled out GOLDEN VALLEY VINEYARDS. Parking in front of the winery, she reached in the back seat for the wide-brimmed, sombrerolike straw hat she always kept in the car. Pushing her amber blond hair back from her forehead, she set the hat squarely on her head and tied the strings under her chin to hold it securely in place. Even this late in the afternoon she needed protection, for the California sun had already bleached the hair that framed her face from its usual deep honey color to a shade as pale and luminous as vintage champagne. As she got out of the car she glanced at the spike-heeled, shiny patent pumps she was wearing. They were new and she hated to scuff the toes, but unless she went to the house to change she would have to risk it. With a shrug, she pulled at the skirt of her blue dress, which outlined the curve of her hips. Sitting for more than an hour on the vinyl bucket seat had made the light summer fabric cling to her body.

She caught sight of Charlie Cartwright watching her through the front window of the winery office. Raising her hand, she waved to the sandy-haired man who was her father's chief winemaker. He waved back and she turned away and walked toward the gate to the vineyards. She kept to the main path, which more or less divided this area of the vineyard closest to the wine storage buildings into two equal sections. She was careful to keep to the center of the walk where the ground was packed firm and worn smooth from use so she would not brush her feet against any loose gravel that could mar her new shoes. After a short distance she angled off to the right, following a slightly narrower footpath between rows of vines which were trained along poles and wires and now, late in the summer, hung heavy with clusters of pale-skinned green grapes.

Rounding a row of low, staked vines, Gayle's legs brushed against the back of a man who was squatting on his heels examining the low hanging clusters of grapes. He rocked back on his heels when her leg touched him, but he didn't lose his balance.

"Oh," she gasped, surprised.

He gave her only a brief glance, then continued his scrutiny of the vine without uttering a word.

"What are you doing?" Gayle's voice rose in vexation and she stared at the crouching man. She had never seen him before and since he was not in jeans or khakis he was apparently not one of the vineyard workers. Her blue eyes narrowed in a frown of irritation. Visitors to the vineyard were limited to guided tours at specific times and certainly never left unattended or allowed to touch the vines.

The man at her feet ignored her and, cradling his large hand under a cluster of grapes, he removed a single grape, rolled it between his fingers slowly, and then put it in his mouth. She stared at every motion of his fingers in a kind of fascinated horror.

9

"You—you're eating our grapes," she accused him angrily.

"Tasting them, *señorita*," he replied. He sprang to his feet with lithe ease and now stood towering over her. "It is an acceptable practice done to determine the ripeness of the grape." There was a hint of cool superiority in his voice, and he had only a trace of a very attractive accent.

Gayle looked up into the darkly handsome face of this tall man whose thick black hair swept back from a wide, intelligent forehead. "I know all about ripe grapes," she said caustically. "You *are* trespassing, you know that don't you?"

"This is a vineyard, not the Garden of Eden, so the fruit is not forbidden," he countered glibly. "And certainly we have established as well that it is a grape I have picked, not an apple." A mocking smile twisted the corners of his mouth.

"What gives you the right to come in here and eat these grapes—taste, or whatever you called it?" Gayle's voice now shook with anger.

His lips compressed into a thin line. "I might ask you the same question. Exactly what are *you* doing here?" His bold black eyes swept over her from head to toe and then returned to rest imperiously on her upturned face.

Seething inwardly at this man's insolence, her eyes flashed with defiance. "I belong in this vineyard—I work here."

"In that dress—and those shoes?" One dark brow quirked as he let his amused gaze travel slowly over her a second time. "Frivolous American females," he sneered under his breath.

Gayle, however, did not fail to hear his contemptuous words and she longed for a scathing retort to hurl in his arrogant face. Instead, she said, speaking her words with a deliberate calm she hoped would give them a sound of authority, "I'm asking you to leave this vineyard right now, and if need be I shall go get the owner to force you to do so." She turned her back on him and began to walk away.

"I can save you the trouble, for I assure you that Stewart Eberly will never ask me to leave his vineyard," he called after her, a ring of conviction in his deep voice.

The mention of her father's name startled her. She hesitated a minute with her back still to the stranger, then slowly turned around and walked back. "You know Stewart Eberly—personally, I mean?"

"I do," he answered, crossing his arms across his chest. "It is at his invitation that I am here."

She studied him carefully in the light of this revelation. He was a striking man and his firmly set mouth and strong jawline gave his features a look of arrogant power which matched the physical power of his body. "Wh–why didn't you tell me you were acquainted with the owner of Golden Valley Vineyards?"

"You didn't bother to ask," he answered curtly.

Nervously, she fingered the strings that held her hat. Who was this man? If he were a friend of her father's, or a business acquaintance, she supposed she had been rude to him. But he, in turn, had behaved in an irritating manner and she had the feeling he deliberately hadn't explained his reasons for being here. She glanced at him once more. He was ruggedly good looking, she would have to give him that, and there was a casual elegance to his smooth brown-leather walking boots, expensive, well-cut brown slacks and impeccable white knit shirt, which bore the monogram RSA on the pocket. The initials did not bring a name to her mind. "I wish you had told me this before," she said by way of apology.

"It's of no matter." He shrugged and thrust his hand in his pocket. "I have a good deal more to see here before I meet with Señor Eberly for dinner, and since you say you work here, I'm certain you have duties to see to." His tone was clearly one of dismissal, and without looking at her he pulled a piece of paper from his pocket and began to study it carefully.

Gayle stood still, frowning, and wondering if she shouldn't explain to him who she was.

"Well, run along," he said impatiently, stuffing the paper back in his pocket. "If you were employed in my vineyards I'd see to it you didn't waste so much time."

Gayle gaped at him in surprise. "*Your* vineyards? Why didn't you tell me right off you were a vintner? You could have saved yourself all this argument." She gave an apologetic little laugh.

"The arguing was your doing, not mine," he said impatiently.

"You're not from the valley; I'd recognize you if you were." Tilting her head so she could see his face from beneath her wide hat, she studied him intently. "Where are you located?"

"Mexico," he snapped. "Near Bahía Kino, in Sonora, to fully answer the question." He walked several steps and bent over to examine the grapes of another vine, making it abundantly obvious how anxious he was to be rid of her.

"Mexico . . ." her voice was touched with interest. "Albariza Wines?" she asked, walking down the row of vines to where he now stood. He nodded his head in answer but did not speak. "Then you are associated with Albariza Vineyards, aren't you?"

His dark eyes flashed, his black brows drawn above them in a bar. "I am Ramon Albariza," he declared, stressing his Spanish intonation.

"You—you're—" she stammered, feeling her face flush warmly with chagrin.

"*Sí, señorita*," he slurred his words, flashing his white teeth in an arrogant smile. "And I can see the discovery of who I am has caused your face to flame the color of one of our Mexican poppies." He laughed, taking delight, it seemed, in her discomfort.

She pulled her hat off and fanned her face with the brim, for now she felt hot as well as uncomfortable in this man's presence. He was haughty and insufferable and even if he were the owner of the most extensive vineyards in all of Mexico he needn't be so smug about it. "I regret asking you to leave the vineyard, of course," she said, pushing her hair back from her flushed face. "And if you had simply informed me who you were and what your business was here at Golden Valley, I would have been more gracious." Deliberately, she punctuated her words with her most charming smile to mask the dislike she felt for his condescending attitude. "Why are you here in the Napa Valley?" She made her tone as pleasant as she could.

"I wish to acquire a vineyard in California."

"Why?"

He eyed her, his lips tight. "Why not?"

13

Gayle found his dark gaze disconcerting. "With all you have in Mexico, I—I find it surprising. Wouldn't you more or less be competing with yourself?"

"I see it as advantageous both production and market wise," he said wryly. "But then, you couldn't understand the ramifications and I haven't the time nor the inclination to explain." He stuck his hand in his pocket and brought out the paper he'd looked at earlier. Without allowing her an opportunity to pursue the subject further, he began to walk ahead, glancing at the paper as he moved down the row of grapevines. He paused and studied the paper again. "Say," he called to her, "from this diagram Eberly drew for me, I take it the *pinot noir* grapes are down and to the left of these *chenin blanc*. Do you know if that's right?"

"Of course I do." She walked between the vines to catch up to him, her high heels sinking deep into the well-cultivated soil. "The 'black grapes' are about three hundred yards to the left." She pointed her finger toward the area. Before he could stride away again she continued. "Why are you looking so carefully at the different varieties of vines here?" She ran her hand under the back of her hair, lifting it off her neck. Not only did she feel uncomfortably hot, but now an uneasy feeling gave a prickling sensation along the back of her neck. "Golden Valley Vineyard isn't up for sale—in fact, I don't know of any place in this section of the valley that is on the market at present. Nothing around St. Helena, that is—" She was breathless from throwing words at him so fast.

"Look, *señorita*," he waved her aside with a negative gesture of his tanned hand, "stop dogging my footsteps. I don't know what your job is here,

the vine sent sugar from leaf to cluster. The sugar content still remained low because July had been somewhat cloudy and cool, but these past weeks of August had been warm and plentifully sunny. This combination of warmth and sun was what the grapes needed for the sugar content to reach the level necessary for fermentation.

She was still thinking about the grape crop as she tossed her straw hat on the back seat and slid behind the wheel of the car. Gazing into the rearview mirror before she started to back away from the winery, her reflection stared back at her. Concentration marked the corners of her eyes with a myriad of tiny lines. Instinctively, she reached for her dark glasses. It was all here. This was what she wanted. Everything that had happened to her today made her realize it. Since she had graduated from college last year she had been spending several hours each day in the lab observing Charlie blending wines. Now she would tell him she wanted to go to work full time, make a career of it. And why not? Women could be successful winemakers as well as men. She could work here at Golden Valley with her father and Charlie and learn all the skills. Charlie was one of the best enologists anywhere and he would teach her, she knew he would. She smiled inwardly. Who knows? In five years, working with someone like Charlie, she could become a really skilled winemaker. Then if someone *did* take over the Golden Valley vineyards, a vintner who knew the Napa Valley, not a stranger like the overbearing Ramon Albariza, she could then make a career for herself here.

It would take study and hard work. It would take time, too, lots of time, but she could do it. She would earn a place for herself here and be able to see that all the wines which bore the Golden Valley label retained the excellence that was the Eberly tradition.

For the first time that afternoon, she felt a smile move across her lips. Growing and harvesting grapes and making wine, this had beauty and purpose. It had been a part of her life for all of her twenty-two years. It was her heritage and it had meaning for her. She would hold onto it.

Chapter Two

"Hi there, Dad. I'm back." Gayle hurried into the wood-paneled den and greeted the gray-haired man who lounged comfortably in a massive leather up-holstered chair. She sighed. "You look so relaxed with your feet propped up like that, and I've had such a lousy day." Her rapid words formed an accompaniment to the staccato click of her heels as she crossed the parquet floor and bent over and kissed him on the forehead.

"You're back from San Francisco early, aren't you?" He glanced up from the trade journal he had been reading. "Hadn't you planned to stay in and have dinner with Ken? You two have hardly seen each other for a month; I thought this was some kind of reunion."

"I had hoped it would be, but it seems I misjudged things. With Ken, it's out of sight, out of mind." She rubbed her hand across her eyes so her father couldn't see the hurt and humiliation she felt. "We can talk about Ken later." She walked around and sat down on the ottoman. Her father moved his feet to make room for her, setting his magazine aside.

"All right, we'll talk about that later," he agreed with an affectionate smile. "But there's something you *do* want to talk about; I can tell that by the stubborn thrust of that pretty chin of yours. So out with it," he said, reaching for a cigar on the table beside his chair.

"I want to know about Ramon Albariza." Her voice rose, revealing her agitation. "What's he doing here in our vineyards? What's he up to anyway? Why, do you know, he's out there pulling grapes from the vines and popping them in his mouth like a vulture?" She spoke faster with every question.

"Slow down, honey. When you're worked up you volley words as if they were Ping-Pong balls and your tongue was a paddle." He laughed good-naturedly, then bit the end off his cigar and prepared to light it. "Now what's all this about Señor Albariza?"

"I just came up from the vineyards and that awful man was there acting as if he owned everything in sight!"

Stewart Eberly frowned. "He's my guest, Gayle, and I hope you weren't rude to him. I'm afraid, however, judging from your attitude now, you were none too gracious." Puffing on his cigar, he regarded her with fatherly tolerance.

"He was the rude one, Dad. And I certainly didn't enjoy watching some arrogant stranger manhandle our grapes!"

"There's no more respected name in the wine industry than his, honey. And I know you've been

20

around a vineyard long enough to have heard of Albariza Wines. I hardly think the grandson of the man who produced the finest sherry in all of Spain would harm the vines of a fellow vintner, do you? Besides, I gave him my permission to look around all he wanted."

She pushed her hands restlessly through her hair. "Dad, you—you scare me with that kind of talk. You—you—" Her voice broke. "You can't possibly be thinking of selling Golden Valley to him?"

He contemplated her worried face with cool gray eyes. "As a matter of fact—yes, I am. I should have told you before that I intended to sell when I came up with the right buyer. I guess I didn't figure on that happening quite so soon as this," he added by way of an apology.

"But why? I don't understand." She shook her head in disbelief.

"I'm sixty-three years old, honey." He pursed his lips and blew out a thin stream of cigar smoke. "It's time for the old man to quit."

"What does age have to do with it? Why, you're the best vintner in the entire valley and you know darn well you could handle this vineyard until you're eighty." She wrinkled her nose at him and the corners of her blue eyes slanted upward beguilingly. "Ninety, even, if you put your mind to it."

"I could, but I don't want to," he said sadly. "I want to retire, and Ramon Albariza can make that possible for me." He leaned back in his chair, his manner one of relaxed contentment. "The offer he's made exceeds my highest expectations and, what's more, I can depend on him to keep the Golden Valley standards of excellence intact and also retain my label." His gray eyes held the warm shine of pewter as he spoke. "The wines I've established won't lose the identity I gave them, and that means more even than the money to me."

"Humph—I wouldn't count on it. Your Mexican friend doesn't impress me as a man who would let anything he touched have any identity but his own." Sarcasm edged her words. "He's insufferably arrogant."

"I disagree, Gayle," he said quietly. "But then, it really isn't all that important now, is it?" Placing his cigar in a glass ashtray, he looked at her, giving her an indulgent smile. "Why should you care, sweetheart?"

Leaning toward him, her eyes wide and luminous, she said, "Oh, but I do care. I really do. I think—that is, I *know*—I truly know now that I want to learn winemaking. I'm serious, Dad. I mean to make a career of it and I need you—and Charlie—to teach me right here at Golden Valley." An urgent pleading sound had come into her voice and her eyes sparkled with excitement.

"You're going to be much too busy running a house for that successful young lawyer of yours to have time for any career in winemaking," he said, making light of her intentions.

"I *will* have time," she interrupted him, her eyes sober and her face pinched with sadness. "That's a big part of it—I need a career to fill my time." She sucked in her breath. "That's what I've been trying to tell you."

Her father straightened his back against the chair and moved his feet off the cushioned ottoman to the floor. "What's wrong Gayle?" Concern filled his voice. "This morning, when you left, I was sure you'd come home from seeing Ken today and tell me you two had made some definite plans for your future."

"I thought so too." She shook her head sadly, her eyes brimming with tears. "But I was entirely wrong, as it turned out." She turned her face away from her father's probing eyes. "Like I said before, out of sight, out of mind, with Ken, and with him in San Francisco all summer and me here, we drifted apart. In fact, Ken did more than drift." She didn't try to keep the bitterness out of her voice.

"What are you telling me, honey?" Leaning toward her, he brushed a tear from her cheek.

Squaring her chin, she turned to face her father, her lips trembling as she spoke. "Ken told me today that he's joining a well-established law firm in the Bay area and he's going to marry the daughter of the senior partner. It seems he's chosen a package deal for himself." Her voice broke in a shuddering sigh and she laced her shaking fingers together tightly in her lap.

The muscles of Stewart Eberly's face tightened, drawing his mouth into a firm line. "Blast!" He fired the word through clenched teeth. "Blast him for hurting you." He took both of Gayle's hands in his. "What can I say, honey? Are you OK?" He spoke quietly, but his voice was heavy with emotion.

She welcomed the warm strength of her father's hands, now pressing hers firmly, reassuringly. "I'll be OK, Dad. I just need a little time." A tear clinging to her lashes, she blinked and closed her eyes for a brief second. Shrugging, she added, "I think in the end I'll discover Ken did me a favor." She paused again, searching for words to explain her feelings to her father. "I never would have belonged in the corporate picture with Ken. I began to see that this afternoon. I belong here, here where things are familiar and feel right to me, working in the vineyard —with you, Dad. That's what I need. It's what I want."

Stewart Eberly's solemn eyes were intent on her face. "It never occurred to me you'd take a serious interest in the vineyard." A troubled frown lined his forehead. "I want to help you, you know that. We'll work it out, whatever you want to do, but think about it. You're upset now, and you need a little time." He patted her hands, then laced his fingers through hers as he used to do when she was a child. The tender, caring gesture touched her. She pressed her lips firmly together and swallowed hard to push back the surge of emotion that threatened to choke her. "Give this time, Gayle. You can be mighty impulsive, you know." He shook his head, a grave look in his narrowed eyes. "I hope you're not going to react so strongly that you block this sale for me."

She jerked her hand from his, startled by his words. "What do you mean—block it? How could I?"

"One third of Golden Valley is in your name, you've always known that. It was split three ways, between your mother, you and me. Your mother's share reverted to me when she died two years ago." He seemed to let his shoulders sag back against his chair as he spoke, his eyes clouding over with memories.

"That was for tax reasons, Dad, I know all of that. It's not really mine, and of course I won't upset anything for you." Standing up, she walked over to the windows, which looked out to the row of low hills which formed a background for the vineyards. "I only wish you were selling to someone from the valley, someone who knew us and might let me stay and work for them."

"I've already made a verbal commitment to Ramon." He paused. "I didn't figure on objections from you," he added regretfully. "Your share is yours, however, to do with as you will."

"What do you think your Mr. Albariza would say if I asked to hold onto my third? Would that ruin the deal for you?" Turning, she faced her father.

"I don't know. He wants these vineyards because we're the fourth largest in the valley and his aim is to control an even larger operation here than he does in Mexico."

"Can he?"

"In five or six years, I expect he can. I know he's hoping to deal with the Trevillo brothers, and if he's able to buy them out and has the Golden Valley, too, he'll become the biggest wine producer in the valley. Ramon is a very ambitious man, Gayle. I think he views himself as head of an Albariza conglomerate that will link his Mexican wines with both California and New York wineries plus, of course, the fine sherries from Spain where the Albariza family started in the wine business." He shrugged, then rubbed his hand across his chin. "Yes, I'd venture to say that gentleman can do just about anything he sets his mind to."

"I don't doubt that he's a shrewd businessman, but I'd never call him a gentleman. From what *I* saw of him, he's entirely without manners and thoroughly offensive." The antique walnut shelf clock made a pinging sound and Gayle was surprised to notice the spidery black hands marking six o'clock. "Where are you taking Mr. Albariza for dinner?" she asked her father.

"I made reservations at the Wine Country Inn for seven forty-five. Why don't you join us and act as hostess for me?" He gave her a brief smile. "Perhaps, if you got to know Ramon, you'd discover he does possess some agreeable qualities."

"I doubt that, and I'm in no mood to spend an entire evening with such an unpleasant companion." She started to leave the room.

"If you're as serious about working here in the vineyard as you say you are, you'd better come along with us. Albariza has assured me he'll keep everyone on here who's been working for me." He settled back in his chair and reached for his cigar again.

"What good would it do? I'm not actually on the payroll, and besides, I'd be willing to bet he wouldn't have a woman working for him under any circumstances."

"You could make a deal with him," her father challenged her.

His words stopped her and she hesitated in the open doorway. "What kind of deal?" Her blue eyes narrowed in a look of speculation.

At that moment the doorbell rang, two chiming tones reverberating from the vestibule through the open archway to the rooms beyond. "That will be Albariza." Stewart Eberly rose from his chair, cigar in hand.

"Look, Dad," Gayle said quickly, "you get the door and I'll go change for dinner. I've decided I do want to go to dinner with you two after all." She pushed her pale hair off her forehead, pressing her fingers firmly against her temples. "I think I have a plan, so don't tell him anything about me. I want it to be a surprise." She smiled at her father. "He doesn't know who I am, and in the vineyard he took me for a guide or possibly a bookkeeper here at the winery." The door chimes sounded again and Gayle fled up the stairs as her father walked through the entryway to open the door to his guest.

In her bedroom, Gayle quickly undressed and as she ran her bath water she swept her blond hair up on top of her head and fastened it with bobby pins. Stepping into the tub, she wished she had more time. She needed to figure out the best way to approach a man like Ramon Albariza. Quite obviously he didn't like women very much; that fact had been made abundantly clear to her by his actions in the vineyard. Plus, he had formed a negative opinion of her during their first meeting. What was it he had said? "Frivolous American females," wasn't that it? Well, she would just have to find a way to make him change that opinion, at least as far as she was concerned.

The warm water soothed her, seeming to dissolve the sharp edges of her tension. The temptation to linger in the pleasantly scented water was hard to resist, but she knew she should join her father and his difficult but somehow intriguing visitor without delay. She bathed quickly, then skillfully applied her makeup and sprayed cologne lightly on her neck and shoulders.

She moved to the closet, looking for something appropriate to wear. "Frivolous." The word of the disdainful Ramon Albariza echoed in her ears again and she pushed aside a feminine turquoise sundress with matching jacket in favor of a dress with a slim skirt and simple round neckline. Fashioned in a soft, clinging material, the dress was the color of sand when touched by warm summer sunlight. Looping two long gold chains around her neck, Gayle took a minute to look at herself in the long mirror on the closet door. Satisfied with her image, she slipped her feet into slender-heeled, bone-colored sandals and buckled the narrow strap. With a final glance in the mirror, she hurried from the bedroom.

As she descended the staircase she could hear the voices of the two men coming from the living room. She was glad her father was serving cocktails there rather than in the den, for the wide expanse of glass which formed the north wall of the spacious living room looked out on a terraced garden surrounding a kidney-shaped swimming pool. Now, in the rose and yellow haze of the summer sunset, the garden appeared bathed in a subtle radiance, and the blue water in the pool looked cool and tranquil. Such a scene, she thought, should instill serenity in the soul of any man, even one as belligerently acquisitive as this arrogant vintner from Mexico.

"There you are, Gayle," her father greeted her. "Ramon, I believe you've met my daughter," he said, gesturing toward her, highball glass in his hand.

Gayle thought she saw a split-second spark of annoyed surprise flash in Ramon's black eyes before an enigmatic smile touched his mouth.

"Yes, it would seem I have," he said tersely, without enlarging on their earlier encounter. He eyed her briefly, but she had the certain impression that nothing about her escaped his critical appraisal. She had expected him to resent the fact that she had not told him in the vineyard who she was, but he was acting as if it didn't matter to him one way or the other. He seemed neither impressed to discover who she was nor chagrined by his earlier rude treatment of her. Perversely, though his earlier anger had angered her, now she found herself irritated by his refusal to react.

"What can I get you to drink?" her father asked, his words sounding loud in the sudden silence that had filled the room.

"I'll get myself a glass of white wine, if there's time before we leave for dinner."

"Of course there's time. But you stay and talk with Ramon. I'll get it for you." He walked from the room before she could protest.

She could feel the other man's eyes following her as she walked the length of the room and took a chair in front of the wide windows. "Did you find what you expected in our vineyards?" she asked.

"I've found even more here at Golden Valley than I had counted on," he answered, taking a seat opposite her at one end of a low sectional sofa.

There was a hint of irony in his low voice and she wondered if he were making his own cryptic little joke. She could not see his expression to tell, however, for he lowered his head and leaned forward to place his glass on an elongated oval coffee table.

"My father tells me you wish to produce Albariza Wines here in California as well as in New York State, Mexico and Spain. I now understand those *ramifications* you spoke of earlier." She pointedly stressed the word, for she was still smarting from his implication that she had no business acumen.

He rubbed his tanned hand along his jaw. "I take it you know, then, that your father has agreed to sell me his vineyards?"

Gayle nodded. "It appears I was mistaken this afternoon when I insisted the Eberly family business was not on the market. I regret Dad's decision, and if there was any way I could convince him not to sell, I would." She didn't look at Ramon as she spoke, instead she gazed through the window at the garden, now purple shadowed in the twilight.

At that moment her father returned. "Golden Valley's own *chenin blanc,* properly chilled and decanted," he said, handing her the glass of wine.

"Thank you, Dad." She took the long-stemmed crystal glass from his hand and studied the pale amber liquid for a moment before tasting it. "This is from 1978," she commented as she held the glass up to the light. "I know it's '78, because the color is the slightest bit deeper than the vintage of any year since '72."

Stewart's eyes crinkled in a smile. "My daughter wishes to become an enologist, Ramon, and she's been acquiring a few firsthand skills from our chief winemaker."

"That's right, you see here in the valley women are readily accepted in this field." Gayle appeared to be totally absorbed in contemplating her glass of wine, but was actually watching the Mexican to see his reaction to the challenge in her words.

"Interesting," he murmured, but the expression on his handsome face denied that he found it so.

"I'm counting on being able to take over Charlie Cartwright's job here one day." Gayle raised her chin in stubborn determination. "I admit I'm just an apprentice right now, but I intend to acquire the knowledge and the skills. Give me five years training and experience and I can become an enologist capable of taking charge of Golden Valley wines." She knew she was boasting, perhaps even exaggerating, but she had no intention of letting Ramon's belittling intimidate her.

"Are you implying that Cartwright is going to another winery?" Ramon ignored Gayle and addressed his question to her father.

"No, of course not." Stewart Eberly shook his head. "But when this year's grape harvest is over and the wine in barrels—well, that seems like the right time for me to step down and put Charlie in charge here. He knows every aspect of the operation and the workers respect him. He should be the man to take my place." His keen eyes studied the Mexican to determine the reaction to his words. "I hope you'll agree to this, Ramon; I feel strongly about it."

"I have no objection whatsoever. Your operation is smooth here and I intend to keep it that way." Ramon picked up his glass. "We'll drink to that, Stewart."

Gayle saw her father's face relax in a satisfied smile as he lifted his glass in agreement. She cleared her throat. She was thoroughly piqued by Ramon's maddening disregard of her, and her father's seeming determination to ignore her ambitions hurt as well. "Well then," she raised her voice. "Since you have no objection to Charlie Cartwright being in charge of the vineyards, how do you feel about my being one of the lab workers?"

"No offense meant, *señorita,* but as I see it there is no place for a woman in the wine industry." His smile was deprecating.

"Perhaps you should make an effort to see it differently, Mr. Albariza," she countered cooly. "A woman can contribute the same degree of excellence to winemaking as a man. That fact has already been demonstrated at several of the wineries here in the valley."

"Drink your wine, Gayle," her father interrupted her. "We'll be leaving for dinner soon."

Obediently, she took a sip of the pale golden liquid and rolled it on her tongue, a glint in her blue eyes. "By the way, did Dad tell you that one third of Golden Valley is in my name?" She gave him a sidelong smile. "So it seems I have a place of sorts in your masculine wine industry after all, even if it's only to put my name on a portion of these vineyards."

Stewart Eberly shot a censuring look at his daughter. Gayle in turn lifted her glance to meet the cool gaze Ramon fixed on her. As his eyes narrowed in thoughtful speculation, she had the distinct feeling that this new knowledge of her partial control of Golden Valley was more than a minor annoyance to him.

"I had not known this, but, of course, I'm not surprised. You did tell me this afternoon that the vineyards belonged in Eberly hands and now I learn that that includes your own small and graceful ones, *señorita*." He nodded his head briefly. "Surely you will permit me to call you Gayle, now that it seems we're to be partners of a sort?" He smiled politely, but his tone lacked any real warmth and his black eyes were glacial.

Her father stood up abruptly. "Get your jacket, Gayle," he said firmly. "It's cooler now that the sun is down. Ramon and I will wait for you in the car."

She knew she had displeased him with her behavior. He had expected her to act as a gracious hostess for him and instead she had deliberately antagonized his guest, and all because she found the Mexican's arrogantly aloof manner infuriating. Ramon Albariza acted as if whatever he desired to own was his by divine right. Well, not her share of Golden Valley! She had no intention of handing over her one-third interest without some compromise on his part. He was not going to take her chance of doing what she wanted to do away from her. Somehow, she would find a way to make Ramon allow her to work in the winery. Given time and training, she knew she could become a skilled winemaker, and she intended to have that time and training, she thought, as she walked quickly from the living room to the wide foyer. Cinching her belt a bit tighter around her slender waist, she picked up the yellow sweater she had left draped over the banister. Placing it around her shoulders, she walked determinedly out the front door to the car.

On the surface, it seemed that the three of them were sharing a congenial meal together. Stewart Eberly managed things adroitly; as soon as they were seated and their order taken, he took charge of the conversation. Gayle knew her father was still upset with her and his tension was obvious, at least to her, for he now kept hold of the reins, turning the subject away from business and onto pleasant social banter. "I understand Bahía Kino is a popular area for deep-sea fishermen," he said to Ramon.

Gayle listened while maintaining a wary detachment. She kept wondering when and how this strongly compelling man would again bring up the subject of her partial ownership of the vineyards. When he did, should she acquiesce without further argument, knowing that was what her father wanted? Did she dare oppose the arrogant vintner from Mexico and attempt to use her one-third interest as a means by which to force him to allow her to work at the winery? She winced inwardly. There was actually no contest involved, for her father's interests were paramount, but still she was determined to strike a bargain with Ramon Albariza. She would prove to him she was not the typical "frivolous American woman."

As if he had read her mind, while the three of them were waiting for dessert to be served, Ramon turned his full attention to her. "I am returning to Mexico tomorrow and I had hoped to reach an agreement among the three of us tonight." His manner was affable and he inclined his head toward her and allowed his arm to rest along the back of her chair. "You know, of course, that I wish to buy your share of Golden Valley as well as your father's." His eyes gleamed darkly into hers and she found herself staring into his strong face, acutely conscious of the magnetic masculinity which seemed to radiate from him. "Will you turn over your share into my hands?" he asked.

"Will you give me a job in the winery if I do?" Deliberately, she kept from looking toward her father. She was on her own in this and she needed to cling to what bit of courage she possessed in order to express her desires. "I want to work full time and learn everything I need to know to become a top-notch winemaker." She turned her eyes from his and ran her tongue over her dry lips.

A muscle twitched in his cheek as he answered her. "What makes you believe you could acomplish that goal?"

His words made her feel defensive. "I lack experience, but I know I have the skills. I've been working with Charlie Cartwright since I graduated from college a year ago."

"You've worked with the chief winemaker daily on an eight to five basis?" He quirked an eyebrow at her and his words held an amused tone of disbelief.

"Well, perhaps not on quite that regular a schedule." Gayle twisted the gold chains at her neck, determined to keep calm and not allow him to see how nervous he was making her.

"I didn't think so." His smile mocked her. "Don't you mean that you took up winemaking as a little hobby, something to occupy you when you weren't caught up in your social pursuits?"

"Why do you refuse to believe I'm serious about this?" she asked, feeling her body tighten in anger. She really disliked everything about this difficult man. "I assure you, this job is vital to me."

"I thought you career oriented American girls sought glamorous positions in metropolitan cities," he said, derision still marking his voice. "You won't be satisfied working all day in a winery."

"You don't know me, Mr. Albariza. I will be entirely content." She continued to finger the chains at her neck.

"Perhaps I *don't* know you, but I *do* know the whims of women, and you American women are never content for long with one place or one activity."

"Are you telling me I can't work in a winery when one third of it is mine?" Gayle pushed the words past the dry tightness that now constricted her throat.

"One third of it will not be yours, for I shall acquire one hundred percent of Golden Valley or I'll own none of it." As he spoke, his white teeth gleamed in a cold smile.

"Then I hope you own none of it!" She threw the

35

words at him in anger and their eyes met, blue fire clashing against black granite. She was aware of her father's sharp intake of breath.

"Gayle!" Stewart Eberly's tone was a reprimand.

She rubbed her hand across her forehead, surprised to feel that, though her skin was slightly damp with perspiration, her face felt cold. An icy shiver ran through her on seeing the frown of disapproval in her father's gray eyes. How tired he looks, she thought, and the realization struck her that since her mother's death two years ago her father had aged beyond his sixty-three years.

"I'm sorry, Dad. Don't be concerned; I won't make waves," she said quietly. "But in a fair business deal, it should be a condition of the sale of Golden Valley that I be given an opportunity to serve at least a brief apprenticeship." Lifting her chin, she looked squarely at Ramon again. "Don't you agree, Mr. Albariza?"

Ramon's face hardened. "Like all American women, the Señorita Eberly stops at nothing to achieve her own desires." The soft slurring of his accented voice did not lessen the derision in his words.

"You're achieving one hundred percent of your own desires," she mocked him. "All I'm asking is a job and a chance to prove myself." Tilting her head in a challenging angle, she narrowed her eyes and smiled tauntingly. "What have you got to lose? You can always fire me."

Ramon's rapier sharp eyes probed hers, and she felt something ominous in the moment of silence between them before Ramon spoke again. "An apprentice must serve under a master craftsman for a stipulated period and in the area designated." He spoke each word slowly, as if emphasizing their meaning to a recalcitrant child. "You may, then, return to Mexico with me tomorrow and work six months in my winery with me." He paused, considering her thoughtfully. "At the end of that time, if you wish to continue, and if I find you show sufficient aptitude, I will allow you to return and work at Golden Valley as a winemaker."

Her head spun at the impact of his words. She couldn't believe his unexpected capitulation to her wishes. Why this sudden reversal? Was it some kind of trick? Did he think she would refuse because he stipulated that she must first work in Mexico with him? She could feel the electrifying tension that was passing between them. The idea of six months in his disturbing presence was far from appealing, but still, she would certainly enjoy proving him wrong in his opinion of her.

"You don't look as if you like the idea. I think you don't trust me to make a fair evaluation of your capabilities."

"On the contrary, my father tells me you're a man of honor in the industry," she answered him, coming out of the jumble of her thoughts. "Therefore, I'm sure you will judge me on the progress I make and the skill I develop, regardless of my sex." She extended her hand. "Shall we shake on that, Mr. Albariza?"

"Ramon," he corrected her, taking her hand firmly in his. "You and I will work together making Albariza Wines, Gayle, since it is your wish to do so. But do not expect my operation in Mexico to be the same as what you have known here in California." A half smile curved his mouth but did not touch his eyes. She wondered if he were issuing a warning to her that, although he was giving in to her request, he had no intention of making any part of it easy for her. She sensed it was an odd victory for her, if indeed it was a victory at all. She had managed to get a job for herself, but to have only six months to prove herself, and to have to do it in a remote area of Mexico beneath the disapproving eyes of this strange but somehow fascinating man, might well prove to be her most challenging undertaking ever. At least she would be deeply involved in learning about winemaking and too busy to dwell on her personal misery over losing Ken. She flushed, aware that her hand still remained in Ramon's. Quickly, she jerked it away to escape the warm pressure of his fingers gripping hers. There was an amused glint in his eyes as he continued to study her intently and his appraisal made her self-conscious. What was he thinking? His expression, though inscrutable, still gave her the feeling that he was considering ways to make it as difficult as possible for her to achieve her goals. This man possessed an unbending attitude toward women in the industry and, indeed, he appeared totally intolerant of American women wherever they might be. Suddenly, and for the first time, apprehensive, she was not at all certain that she should go to Mexico. Working with Charlie Cartwright here in the Napa Valley was one thing, leaving the country for six months to work closely with this compelling Mexican was another. She looked quickly to her father. Wouldn't he have reservations about her leaving the valley? If only he would change his mind and refuse to sell Golden Valley to this foreigner. It would be so perfect if he would decide to keep control of the vineyard for at least another year. Was there any way she could persuade him to do this? She implored him silently with her eyes, but Stewart Eberly seemed unaware of the conflicts churning inside her. He sat, relaxed, and seemingly content, with a smile easing the tired lines at each side of his mouth. As she gazed at him, he picked up his fork and took a large bite out of the slice of golden crusted apple pie the waitress had just placed in front of him. She reached for her water glass, regretting that she had ordered dessert, for suddenly the thought of eating had lost all appeal.

Chapter Three

The following morning she began to pack, sorting through her closet in a frenzy of indecision. She was going to Mexico to work, not for a romantic, idyllic vacation, so what she needed were practical, easy care, cool clothes to wear on the job. She could just imagine Ramon's scathing remarks if she appeared with vast amounts of luggage, so with this in mind she set out only one large suitcase and one smaller one. She would take what these would hold and that would have to suffice. Taking her time and choosing with care, she discovered she had enough space left to put in two impractical and ultrafeminine dresses. She was delighted, and she smiled, thinking she would be prepared in case of a *fiesta*, and surely, in Mexico, the harvesting of the grapes would call for a gala celebration. As she folded each garment carefully, she tried to picture the lordly Ramon participating in the capricious revelry of a wine festival.

Laughing inwardly, she decided she would require a very different escort than her unbending employer for such a fiesta and, indeed, would prefer someone else.

From his sphinxlike way of imparting a minimum of information, Gayle knew only that Ramon would pick her up at eleven that morning, so at ten till the appointed hour she had her luggage downstairs and was ready to walk out the front door when he arrived.

"I see you do own a sensible pair of shoes after all," he greeted her, taking note of her trim navy pumps and then making a slow, sweeping assessment of her navy linen suit with its matching sleeveless vest worn over a v-necked, tailored white blouse.

His appraisal seemed to give him a certain amount of satisfaction, but she also suspected he was making fun of her about the shoes. "I have a very complete wardrobe and I always wear what I think will be required," she informed him primly, and feeling her statement more than covered the subject, she dismissed it. Determined to start this day off pleasantly, she smiled, and asked, "Does our plane leave from Santa Rosa or do we have to go down to San Francisco first?"

"Santa Rosa," he answered without elaborating. And picking up her suitcases, he carried them out to the car. Gayle didn't wait for him to open the car door for her, but walked around and got in the front seat while he put her luggage in the trunk. Ramon made no attempt to converse with her as they drove away from the house, along the curving gravel road that wound past the winery and the vineyards for four miles before reaching the highway. He certainly could be a man of few words, she thought, and she

wondered if he found casual conversation unneces-
sary with everyone or just with her. As if he sensed
what she was thinking, he shot her a brief glance out
of the corner of his eye.

"I never thought you'd agree to come to Mexico
with me, Gayle."

"Why not?" She gave him a long look, studying
his handsome profile.

"You take such pride in your own Golden Valley
vineyards and you have this feeling of belonging
there; I thought nothing would tear you away."

"I had the distinct impression that you didn't give
me a choice."

"No, I didn't," he stated flatly. He pulled the car
into the left lane, accelerating to pass the blue sedan
in front of them. She had the feeling he was deliberately refusing to look at her.

"You hoped that by telling me I had to work in
Mexico you would make me decide not to accept
your offer. You counted on my backing off, turning
you down, didn't you?"

"I hoped you would, yes." He kept his eyes
forward, as if his only interest was in the road ahead.

Gayle noticed how the forward thrust of his chin
accented the taut chords of his neck. How savagely
he resents being thwarted, she thought, feeling a
degree of satisfaction. "Why are you telling me
this?"

"Because I never worked with a woman before
and I regret having to start now." Ramon's strong
mouth hardened. "The truth is, I've had enough of
women interfering in my life with their disruptive
ways." The car shot forward as he pressed the
accelerator to accompany the sharp thrust of his
words.

"Well, you and I have something in common after all. You've had enough of women and I've had enough of men." She clipped her words off precisely, as if she were cutting them out with scissors. "Why don't we try to work not as a man and a woman, but as two people with a common interest in the wine industry?" She gave him a thin smile.

"Do you think you can do that?"

She frowned at him. "Do what?"

"Manage to think of me as a wine *person* and not as a *man*." His words were laced with male ego.

"I'll force myself. Perhaps if I concentrate my efforts, I'll be able to manage it," she countered glibly.

"I've yet to see a girl who didn't feel she had to prove her attractiveness by testing her charms on each and every man she met, and I don't think you're the exception." He spoke now without inflection, only a cool evenness in his tone.

"Well, we'll just have to wait and see, won't we?" Her voice was lightly sarcastic. "I intend to learn winemaking from you. You are my teacher and I am your student. That is the only basis for our relationship." She shrugged, anxious to dismiss the subject. "That should prove a satisfactory arrangement for both of us."

"Ummm, possibly," he muttered.

They drove for several minutes in silence. Gayle fidgeted in her seat, determined to come up with some neutral topic of conversation that would create a more pleasant atmosphere between them. "Tell me about the flight to Mexico. How long does it take? Do we have to change planes? Do we fly part of the way on one of the Mexican airlines?"

It seemed that her numerous questions did breach

the gap between them, for Ramon smiled at her, relaxing the tense lines around his mouth. "I thought it was about time you started wondering about the trip. And to answer some of your questions, I'd say since it's a clear day it should take us about four and a half hours in a small plane."

She welcomed the pleasantness that now entered his voice, but his statement puzzled her. "What do you mean? I thought all commercial planes were large jets."

"I guess I neglected to tell you, I have my own plane—a Beachcraft Baron. I'll be flying us to Bahía Kino."

Her eyes widened in astonishment. "You—you fly your own plane?"

"Does the idea frighten you?" He sounded amused, and she realized he was enjoying her alarmed reaction.

"I've only flown commercially before," she said, avoiding a direct answer. "I certainly never expected to be flying to Mexico in a private plane."

"And you don't relish the idea much either, I can see that," Ramon mocked her. "Your fears are unwarranted. I've been flying for sixteen years and I've never lost a passenger yet."

Dislike for him blazed anew inside her. She knew he was taking a perverse satisfaction in making her as uncomfortable about this as he possibly could. Taking a deep breath, she pressed her hands together in her lap, deciding to meet him head on. "I'm sure everything you do you do with competence," she said evenly. "It is true, though, that I never expected to be flying in your plane with you as pilot, and I admit I have an uncomfortable feeling about it." Lifting her head and tossing her hair back, she challenged him with cool blue eyes. "If that means I'm afraid, then I guess I must be."

"Look, Gayle, don't be." He spoke quickly, and put his hand on her arm reassuringly. "You needn't be apprehensive with me." This lightning change in his attitude toward her came so unexpectedly that she felt stunned. Why his ambivalent treatment of her? His strong hand still held her arm and the warm pressure was having a strange affect on her. "I admire you, Gayle," he said, after studying her face with his dark expressive eyes. "At least you're honest enough to admit your fears. Most women lie about their feelings." He took his hand away then, and his soft accented voice now took on an edge of bitterness. "It's been my experience that American women are deceitful concerning everything."

"Then I'd say you had shared your experiences with the wrong Americans," she said, rubbing her arm where his hand had been. It was ridiculous, but she was sorry he had withdrawn his hand so quickly. "You wouldn't judge the quality of an entire vineyard on the basis of only one or two vines, would you?"

Ramon either did not care to comment or else he thought she was being flippant. At any rate, he merely shrugged his broad shoulders, then turned into the Santa Rosa airport.

Less than forty-five minutes later, they had finished a quick lunch in the airport coffee shop and Gayle stood watching Ramon inspect the Beachcraft Baron. She was amused because he seemed so intensely concerned about his plane. He checked the engines, fuel, oil, props, landing gear, and then every inch of the plane's surface, making her think of a little boy playing astronaut.

"The way you're fussing over this plane of yours makes me wonder if it will make the trip," she said with a teasing lilt in her voice.

Ramon gave her a condescending smile. "She's a spirited woman, this lovely lady." He patted the side of the fuselage. "Rather like a beautiful courtesan, for she can ravish with her ecstasies, but she also demands the utmost in care. If she's unsatisfied with the attentions she receives, then she rewards her lover with death. So I'm very careful with my inspections."

Gayle wasn't amused any longer, nor impressed with his similes. She walked to the door of the plane. "If you don't mind, I'll wait inside while you finish."

He raised one well-shaped brow. "That's fine, if you really think you want to, but since I fly from the left seat either I get in first or I shall have to crawl across your lap." He gave her a roguish smile. "I don't mind, if you don't."

"I mind," she said, and turned away so she wouldn't have to face the amused laughter Ramon made no attempt to suppress. In fact, he seemed to take delight in the knowledge that she was acutely embarrassed.

A few minutes later, Ramon, seemingly satisfied that the Beachcraft was in order, climbed in first and Gayle followed, taking the seat next to his. Once inside, her earlier apprehension at the thought of flying in a small plane returned. Not wanting to risk further comments from Ramon, she tried to make herself relax. To this end, the comfortable contours of the leather upholstered seat helped, for it fit smoothly to her back, giving support. Her eyes were drawn to the instrument panel full of complicated dials, some fifteen of them stacked over the numerous engine controls. Although she should have found this scientific instrumentation reassuring, somehow the sight was awesome and did nothing to relieve her inner tensions.

Glancing up, she discovered the nicest feature of the plane, the wraparound windshield which appeared to open up the entire sky to her. Perhaps if she concentrated on the serene blue of the heavens and the clear light of the early afternoon sun she would be able to enjoy the flight which lay ahead. Realizing that she was actually holding her breath, she let it out quickly, hoping Ramon hadn't noticed this additional sign of fear.

"Now, if you're ready, let me show you how to fasten your seat belt and shoulder harness."

She heard Ramon's words but before she really knew what was happening, he was leaning over her, his hand brushing her breast as he worked to smooth the broad straps over her shoulders and across her chest. Recoiling from his touch, she pressed her back firmly against the seat, her breathing suddenly erratic. She sensed he was deliberately taking more time than was necessary, but the operation finally ended as he snapped the metal buckles on her seat belt firmly into place. He drew back, then, and studied her intently, an expression of amused indifference on his handsome face.

"I'm only interested in taking precautions for your safety, Gayle. Nothing more, I assure you." One dark brow arched mockingly.

She could feel anger flaming in her cheeks. What conceit he possessed. Did he imagine for a second that she would invite his advances? "I appreciate your concern for my physical well-being." Fury and disdain colored her words.

"Federal aviation regulations require the pilot to make certain the passenger can operate the seat belt," he said. The soft, slurring intonation was exaggerated now in his speech.

"I understand perfectly well how to arrange this contraption, so you needn't bother further. I can handle it myself from here on out." She turned her face away to escape his laughing eyes. Interlacing her fingers, she pressed her hands into her lap and gazed steadily out the window, for she refused to carry this thoroughly inane conversation a step further.

"Baron, three—three—three—Mexican Wine, ready for takeoff." She could hear Ramon asking for clearance from the Santa Rosa tower.

"Baron—triple three—Mexican Wine, cleared for takeoff," rasped from the speaker overhead. Gayle was fascinated by what was taking place. She stared at Ramon as he advanced the throttle levers and the engines crescendoed until they sounded like the scream of a banshee. As the plane accelerated down the runway, Gayle could feel the force of a thousand invisible hands pressing her body into the contours of her seat. She saw Ramon glance at the heading indicator and then scan the other instruments.

"What are you doing now?" she asked, wanting to understand something of what was going on.

"Switching us onto the automatic pilot," he answered, his manner offhand, and she felt quite certain he had no interest in explaining anything further to her. As he moved his hand on the switch, the wings jerked quickly and Gayle caught her breath in fright. Ramon didn't seem to notice, or if he did, he made no comment. His eyes seemed to be intently searching every gauge and dial. She watched his fingers gliding delicately to adjust the knobs and press switches as deftly as a surgeon's. When all was apparently satisfactory, he looked out on his kingdom of sky with a satisfied smile and eyes that sparkled with achievement.

Watching him, Gayle had the feeling that he had escaped into another world, a world where only he and his plane existed. She smiled inwardly at the thought, and for the first time since she had gotten in the plane, she relaxed.

She recalled the words Ramon had used when he requested clearance. "Triple three—Mexican Wine." She remembered now the bold marks on the tail of the plane, the trio of black threes followed by a large M and a W. Mexican Wine, that must be what it stood for. Absently, she rubbed her hand across her chin, smiling to herself. Ramon Albariza would of course choose call numbers and letters for his plane that would identify him with his wine, and he had undoubtedly selected the number three to signify the three elements of fine wine: bouquet, color and taste.

Out of the corner of her eyes she examined Ramon's profile. It would truly seem that the absorbing interest of this ambitious man was the production of the wines that bore his name. Maybe it was this dedication that seemed to set him apart, give him a certain presence, an aura of magnetism and vitality that she found disturbingly intriguing. Whatever it was, she had to admit, he was a man very much in charge of his own life.

The plane now appeared to be climbing rungs of white clouds that laddered the summer sky. When the two-engine Beachcraft leveled off in smooth flight, Ramon commented, "You can loosen your seat belt now, if you like, and be comfortable."

Gayle followed his suggestion and, once free of the restrictions, she crossed one slender leg over the other. She had no intention of attempting to talk to him further as there seemed to be no subject on which the two of them could converse amiably and she did not intend to allow him to mock her again, nor put her down with that arrogant superiority of his. Perhaps with silence they could maintain neutrality between them, she thought, as she angled her head so as not to appear to be looking at his strong-boned face. Though she resented his compelling magnetism, nevertheless, she had to admit that she was fascinated by his striking good looks. His hair was blacker than a starless night and she found the liquid sheen of those dark eyes more than distracting. They made her think of the mirrored surface of a tropical lake that didn't reveal the dangers hidden below.

"I thought all women were curious about where they were going?" Ramon's low voice penetrated the silence. "You haven't asked me a single question about Bahía Kino." He unfastened his own seat belt and slowly rubbed the back of his neck, at the same time leaning toward her, his eyes narrowing in a smile. "I'll wager you're in for several surprises." His voice held a teasingly mysterious note which she found intriguing.

"I'm curious, of course, but I didn't want to bore you with a lot of typical female questions." She raised her eyes to meet his. "I would like you to tell me about your city, though."

He leaned closer, so close that his breath feathered her cheek. "I'll let you know when you bore me, Gayle. That's one thing you can be very sure of."

Her blue eyes widened in surprise and for one breathless moment she thought she glimpsed an unexpected vulnerability in the depths of his eyes. She must have imagined it, for the next instant, with only a slight change of inflection, he said, "Bahía Kino is far from a city, in fact, it is scarcely even a town. It's merely a small, remote, deep-sea fishing village on the west coast of Mexico."

"Is that on the Gulf of California?"

"Yes, but we call it the Sea of Cortez; the water is incredibly blue or green depending on the time of day and the angle of the sun. My house is located so close to the beach you can't escape from the sight and sound of the sea. It might seem monotonous to some, but not to me." He looked at her, and now there was something very human and warm in his expression. "I actually resent the time I have to be away."

"It sounds as if you've found your own paradise."

His jaw tightened and the pleased look vanished. "My paradise, yes—but it will not seem so to you. There are seldom Americans in our area of Mexico, only a few hundred Mexicans and the Seri Indians, who live in the nearby village of Punta Chueca. I'm certain you will find it strange."

"Perhaps at first it will be strange, but from what you've told me, it has to be a fascinating place to live." She crinkled her eyes in a smile. "I'm looking forward to my stay there."

He straightened abruptly and seemed to glare at the instrument panel in front of him. "You'll find it lonely. Americans do it seems—my mother grew to hate it." A harsh note of censure edged his words and the sudden change in his attitude baffled her.

"But—but I thought you said there were rarely Americans there?"

"I said few ever want to live there. Mother refused to live there all the time. She was constantly coming and going, and once she stayed away for most of a year." He pushed the words through clenched teeth in angry condemnation.

"Your mother was an American?" Her voice mirrored her disbelief.

"I can see that raises questions in that woman's mind of yours," he said, lifting a dark brow as he'd done at the vineyard when he had told her so proudly that he was Ramon Albariza. "Needless to say, my Mexican genes predominate. I look like my father. Mother was fair, but with deep violet eyes, and her hair was like yours, the amber color of sherry wine." As he spoke, he reached over and pushed her hair back from her face where it had fallen across her cheek. The timbre of his voice held a tone that was at the same time fierce yet strangely gentle. His words and gesture were so out of character for him, and indeed, these past few minutes of conversation were so far removed from what she had come to expect from him, that she wondered if she could be hallucinating. She could feel the chaotic rhythm of her heartbeat as his eyes penetrated hers with a look that, paradoxically, held both fire and ice. Ramon trailed his fingers across her cheek and his touch was so light that it was like a whisper of air caressing her skin. A fleeting instant and it was over. He pulled his hand away and ran it through his own dark hair, parting it with his strong fingers.

"As I explained to your father before we left this

morning, our area of Mexico is not suitable for an American girl alone." He had adeptly changed the subject from his own heritage to her present situation. "Therefore, Gayle, you will stay at my house, Casa del Mar, and Maria, my housekeeper, will see that everything is comfortable for you." Ramon had resumed his authoritative manner and he spoke of these arrangements with casual indifference, not bothering to ask what her wishes in the matter might be.

She found his ambivalent attitude toward her not only insulting but maddening. Did he regret having mentioned something of his background to her? Being a man who held himself aloof from others, did he intend to maintain the lofty master/unworthy apprentice status between them? That had to be it. Now he was angry that he had revealed anything of himself to her and he was putting her down by disposing of her like she were some itinerant grape picker. She glared at him, her lips pursed in stubborn anger. "Surely I can find another suitable place to stay? I wouldn't dream of imposing on you." The coolness of her voice matched the detachment of his. "I do not want to get in *your way*." She stressed her words to show her anger.

"My house is large, and since a great deal of your time will be spent working at the winery, I doubt there will be much opportunity for you to get in my way. Unless I choose to have it so, that is." His white teeth flashed in an insolent grin. "As a guest at Casa del Mar, I will entertain you at the times and in the manner I shall choose, and I assure you, my dear Gayle, such an attractive addition to the household as you will not prove to be an imposition, but, rather, a charming diversion."

She was incensed, for he was deliberately making fun of her. Putting her hands to her neck, she fingered the vee of her blouse, busying her trembling fingers. It had been a long time since she had wanted to lash out and strike someone, but at this moment she would have found immense satisfaction in slapping Ramon's smug face. Instead, she straightened the front of her vest, ignoring him as if his words were of no significance whatever to her. The last man in the world she would want to entertain her in any fashion was this insufferable egotist. Right now, she didn't need nor want *any* man to complicate her life. She thought of Ken, and a band of pain circled her chest, interfering with her breathing. She crossed her arms across her breasts, as if to shield herself against further hurt, and gazed out the window.

The flight of the plane was so even and smooth it scarcely seemed they were moving at all. In the company of someone other than Ramon, she could actually have found enjoyment in the flight. Certainly the weather was ideal and the sky was a lovely shade of blue, like the shell of a robin's egg. The midafternoon sun gave a crystalline radiance to the atmosphere. Days like this, Gayle thought, were perfect for ripening the grapes. She would have liked to discuss with Ramon how soon his Mexican vines would reach their desired peak. Farther south, and with the dry, hot summer sun, his grapes might well be a month ahead of those in the Napa Valley. It would prove interesting learning about the wines of a different area, and her six months of training in the Albariza winery could prove of enormous value. Smiling inwardly, she thought she might end up being grateful that Ramon had forced her to accept his terms after all, even though she knew he would probably put as many hurdles in her way as he could. He would like nothing better than to dissuade her from her goals, but she would stick it out. Closing her eyes, she let her mind dwell on the immense satisfaction she would experience if, sometime during these next six months, she could even briefly get the upper hand against this high and mighty potentate of the Mexican wine industry. She let out a sigh of utter delight at the thought, and, keeping her eyes closed, she let the buoyancy of the plane lull her into a welcome sleep.

"Gayle, I must disturb your reverie." The low cadence of Ramon's voice brushed against her ear. Turning her head, she opened her eyes, blinking in awareness, and discovered that Ramon's face was so close to hers that for the barest second her forehead had brushed against his lips. "I hated to awaken you," he said, still with his head bent over her. "But we have to land, pass through customs and refuel. We've already crossed the border. You are in my country now," he added, and there was a proud ring to the way he emphasized the final words.

Gayle could feel her heart fluttering like the wings of a captive bird as he leaned even closer. "I believe you wished to handle this for yourself," he said, and, picking up the ends of her seat belt, he placed them in her hands. "So do it quickly." He moved abruptly away, his manner suddenly perfunctory.

She fumbled with the seat belt, then pretended a preoccupation with the shoulder harness. Why was she so flustered?

"Perhaps you do require my help, after all?" He

made a motion as if he would take the shoulder strap from her hand and his eyes sparked with barely concealed laughter.

"No—leave me alone." Her voice rose sharply. "It was twisted, but I have it straight now."

He eyed her for a moment with wry amusement, then straightened in his seat and adjusted a lever on the control panel. The plane began a gradual descent. As they lost altitude, she began to see the patchwork pattern of the countryside below. Suddenly the plane began to bounce up and down like a car driving over a rutted gravel road.

"What's wrong?" Gayle's face paled and she caught her breath in a frightened gasp, all the time pressing her back hard against the leather seat.

"No problem," he shook his head at her. "Nothing is wrong, Gayle. We're in some convexion currents." He looked at her and gestured with his hand. "Simple updrafts and downdrafts—it'll be over in a minute." He gave a soft chuckle. "Relax, fair lady. Remember, you may be safer with me in the air than you'll be when we're on the ground."

Her fingers were trembling as she rubbed them across her lips. Was Ramon teasing her to get her over being frightened, or was there some serious intent to his statement? Under the pretense of easing her body into a more relaxed position, she glanced quickly at his face. His expression was unreadable, which both intrigued and annoyed her.

At the town of Hermosillo, Ramon accomplished the customs clearance with ease. Apparently he was well acquainted with the Mexican officials and they appeared friendly, even obsequious, in their dealings with him. A slight young Mexican, who appeared eager to offer assistance, directed Gayle to a counter where tourist cards were issued. An overweight older man, his face beaded with perspiration, sat on a stool behind the long counter and as she approached he surveyed her in a slow, impertinent manner.

"And you, *señorita*," he drawled. "For what purpose do you come to Mexico and how long do you plan to stay?"

Before she could answer, Ramon moved immediately to stand close beside her, addressing the unpleasant man in easy Spanish.

The official listened with disinterest, his thick underlip pushed forward, giving his heavy jowled face the expression of a fat bullfrog. He took his time replying to Ramon, and when he did, even the soft cadence of the Spanish language did not mask the disparaging crudeness of his attitude. Gayle couldn't understand what exactly he said, but somehow she knew that it was aimed at her and that it was coarse, even vulgar. Ramon's retaliation was fierce, and he pelted the Mexican with a barrage of steel-edged words, the only ones of which she could understand were *vinos de Albariza*—"Albariza Wines."

"Ah, Señor Albariza, *perdón, perdón.*" His large head bobbed rapidly on his short neck and he flushed profusely. Without another second's delay, the visitor's card was issued and extended with a smile and a nod to Gayle. "May the lovely *señorita* enjoy herself in Mexico," he said, and Gayle tried hard not to shudder as she took the card from him.

Circling her waist with his strong arm, Ramon pulled her away quickly and led her out of the building. Once outside, he took his arm away abruptly. "Let's get back to the plane," he said brusquely.

Hurrying after him, she wondered why he was so tense. Breaking into a run to catch up, she then walked at a fast clip to stay abreast of him. "What did that man say to upset you so?" she panted. "And slow down, it's too hot to move so fast." He ignored her question, but he did shorten his steps to some slight degree. "Tell me what he said. I know he was talking about me, and I have a right to know." She looked up at him in breathless expectation.

Ramon stopped abruptly and, grabbing both her arms, held her squarely in front of him. "He was talking about you all right." His eyes swept over her and his fingers tightened on her arms, steadying her, for he had yanked her to a halt so unexpectedly that she had almost lost her balance. She stared up into the hard onyx eyes only inches from her own and felt a sudden throbbing pulse in her throat that threatened to choke her. This close to him, she could see a fine film of perspiration on his forehead and smell the clean masculine scent of his skin mixed with a hint of sandalwood after-shave. A sneer thinned the hard line of his mouth. "That fat idiot wouldn't believe that a girl who looked like you do would come to Mexico with me only to work in my winery."

"Well, that's curious," her eyes widened in surprise. "Why else would you bring me here?" Ramon's nearness created such a disturbing clamor of emotions in her that she spoke without thinking of the implication in her question. The words were no sooner out of her mouth than she regretted them, and she felt the embarrassed flush of her face.

Ramon apparently decided that he had no need to answer her question, for the unspoken answer already hung in the air between them.

He intensified his fierce hold. "Your fair skin and blond hair may well prove an alluring novelty in Mexico, but keep in mind that it is my vineyard and I will not tolerate any disruptive element." He pulled her closer, his blazing black eyes burning into hers. "You're here to learn winemaking, not to play the enticing amber witch. Is that understood?"

The vehemence of his words both appalled and angered her, for she had done nothing that she knew of to incur his outrageous treatment. Furiously, she tried to wrench herself from his grasp, but her efforts proved futile, and she began to shake uncontrollably under the painful pressure of his hands. "Let me go!" she hissed through trembling lips.

"When you can assure me that you and I understand each other concerning my vineyards, Señorita Gayle. Then I will let you go." Once again, that soft, slurring intonation marked his speech, and his anger now was matched by his mockery.

Energized with rebellious courage and determined to stand up to him, Gayle deliberately parted her lips in a provocative smile. "To be labeled enticing and viewed as a disruptive element is quite flattering. I shall take your attitude toward me as a compliment." She realized she was issuing what he would see as a challenge, but at this moment she was too angry to care.

"Take it any way you like," he said tersely. "Only remember, you are now in *my* country, working in *my* vineyards, and everything here will be done the way *I* say it shall be done."

"I know; you've already made that perfectly clear," she shot back sarcastically. "I'm at your mercy—wasn't that how you put it?"

An odd flame leaped in the depths of his dark

eyes. "Exactly! Do we understand each other, *señorita?*"

"Oh, you may be assured, *señor,* I understand you completely." Looking up then, she met his eyes with an unflinching look. Never had any man so inflamed her. It was indignation that was causing her heart to thunder so, nothing more, she told herself. "Now, if you will free my arms, perhaps we can shake on our mutual understanding of *my* place in *your* vineyards."

Ramon's eyes narrowed dangerously, his burning look traveling over her face to rest on her parted lips. Before she realized what was happening, she was crushed savagely against his hard, muscular body. His splayed fingers pressed with unrelenting force against her back, molding her to him.

Shock rippled through her veins as his mouth descended, capturing hers with accurate expertise. Caught off guard, she was at first too surprised to offer any resistance, and then every nerve in her body seemed to come alive under his caress. His lips were persuasive, coaxing a pliant response from her that stunned her. This couldn't be happening. How could this infuriating man so inflame her senses? She had the most unreasonable desire to cling to him. It was insanity. Pressing her hands hard against his chest, she jerked away and turned her face from his.

Now that he was no longer kissing her, she could think more clearly. She was reacting to Ramon only because her pride still suffered from Ken's rejection. That would explain it. She was seeking solace in another man's embrace, seeking to prove to herself that she was still attractive. Lifting her head, she ran her tongue over lips that still throbbed from Ramon's demanding kiss. She knew exactly what was in his mind. He had been demonstrating his dominance over her to prove beyond the shadow of a doubt, that he was master of the situation he had forced her to accept.

She saw the sardonic glitter beneath the dark lashes and then his lips moved in a knowing smile. "Now we understand each other, my little American winemaker."

She ached to protest. She was not *his* anything! But before she could speak, he continued. "We shall get back in the plane now and fly to my vineyard." He took hold of her arm and steered her toward the end of the paved airstrip, where the plane waited, giving her no chance to do anything but follow.

Chapter Four

It was late afternoon when the wheels of the plane touched down at one end of Ramon's vast vineyards, rolling along the slender runway which was bordered by what appeared to be chalky white, coarse sand. However, on closer inspection, Gayle realized that the area surrounding the landing strip was covered with crushed seashells, which shone in the sunlight with a pearlized luster. This wide, white path seemed to be cut right through the center of the vineyards and she was awed by the tremendous area which was covered by row upon row of cultivated vines. Ramon's operation here must be four, even five times more extensive than that of her father's in the Napa valley. With gradually decreasing speed, Ramon taxied the plane up close to a covered structure, which obviously must serve as a hangar for the Beachcraft. As she climbed out, Gayle saw a Mexican wearing a wide straw sombrero striding toward them from the vineyard. When he saw Ramon, the man raised one hand in a salute of greeting.

"Here comes my number one man, Fernando Montoya," Ramon said in way of explanation. "He's in charge of overseeing all the vineyards."

The two of them talked for a few minutes while Gayle watched them from the shadow of the airplane. Although it was five o'clock, the sun still shone down with a bright glare and a furnacelike heat radiated from the sunbaked pavement beneath her feet. She took her sunglasses from her purse and put them on. Glancing again toward the men, she hoped that Ramon would not delay long. She was both tired and miserably hot. During the past few hours she had experienced a potpourri of emotions and she needed an opportunity to relax and sift the events of the day through her mind. There were certain facets of Ramon's personality that baffled her, and she doubted that, even after six months with him, she would ever understand this complex man. She sighed, and pushed aside the damp hair that clung to the sides of her face.

Ramon was frowning darkly as he and the Mexican joined her. "Gayle, this is Fernando." He sounded curt. "You'll see a great deal of him while you are here."

The squarely built middle-aged man removed his wide-brimmed hat and nodded his balding head in an acknowledging bow. "Welcome, *señorita*. May you enjoy your stay here at Albariza vineyards."

"I'm sure I will," she answered, smiling. She liked this pleasant-faced man on sight, and she felt a strong need to have him as an ally here. "I must say, it's an overwhelming sight from the air." She gestured toward the rows of vines. "Much more extensive than where I come from."

"You can see it all in the morning when it's cooler," Ramon cut her off, his voice sharply edged with impatience. "The main building of the winery is about eight hundred yards ahead," he continued brusquely. "Fernando will get the car and our luggage and pick us up there. Come on, Gayle." He began walking away from the plane. Gayle adjusted her bag higher on her shoulder and took several rapid steps to catch up, her shoes making a sharp crunching sound on the shell-strewn roadway.

"Fernando should have had a car down here at the hangar waiting for us, but it seems there's a visitor here this afternoon who interrupted everyone's schedule." His voice mirrored his anger and he glowered as he marched along, almost stabbing the ground with the heels of his boots. "An interfering nuisance disrupting the work here by taking a bevy of ridiculous pictures—it wouldn't have been permitted had I been here." He muttered his complaints more to himself than to her. Unbuttoning the neck of his shirt, he rubbed his hand across his bronzed chest. "The heat is grim this time of year," he said, as he opened his shirt even more. "I apologize that you have to walk in it," he said, seeming to notice her discomfort for the first time.

"It's OK," she said, then paused and glanced up at him. "Since I have on my sensible shoes, that is." She laughed, wanting to lighten his mood. She would have liked to have stopped long enough to wipe the perspiration from her face, but she was afraid to suggest it. Ramon would think she was complaining and she certainly was not going to risk seeing him riled further.

He glanced down at her, the tense lines of his face relaxing slightly. "You're fairly tractable when you're wearing your sensible shoes. Do you know that?" A flash of a smile darted across his face, but just as a meteor marks a midnight sky with an instant glowing streak, then disappears to leave the heavens empty, Ramon's smile vanished as rapidly as it had come, and now his expression was more forbidding than before, as if he resented his earlier easiness with her.

The road swung to the right and inclined gradually to meet beige-colored adobe walls which enclosed the winery buildings. In the center of the wall, black wrought-iron gates opened inward, and above the gates ornate arched grillwork spelled out ALBARIZA WINES. Once inside, Gayle smiled in pleased surprise to discover a colorful plaza inlaid with rust brown Mexican tiles. The area was surrounded by red and white blooming oleander bushes. The profusion of blossoms scented the air with a subtle fragrance. Directly in front of the main building, a flagpole bore two brightly colored banners. In the higher position flew the flag of Mexico, three vertical bars of color—green, white and red. Below it was the sign of Albariza Wines—on a field of gleaming white, the royal blue figure of a matador, his scarlet cape lifted majestically before a charging black bull. How plain, even ordinary, Golden Valley was compared to all of this. Gayle felt an awakening sense of excitement at the thought of working here. There was an exotic quality to this place where the color and flavor of Mexico joined with the Spanish heritage of Albariza Wines. No wonder Ramon spoke of it with such fierce pride. He was, after all, ruler of this kingdom.

She turned to him, wanting to tell him how

impressive this all was, but something stopped her as his tall body suddenly stiffened. She followed his glance to the open doorway of the building just ahead. A tall, perfectly proportioned, auburn-haired girl posed artfully in the doorway, her stance that of an experienced model. The knee-high slit of her white skirt revealed a shapely tanned leg, while the scooped neck of the blouse she wore disclosed more of her golden, satin-smooth skin.

"I'm glad to see you, darling." Coral-colored lips parted in an inviting smile as she greeted Ramon. "I had almost given up hope that you'd get back today." She stepped from the doorway and with slow, catlike grace, moved to meet him.

"Fernando tells me you've not been idle while you waited." His nostrils flared. "You've interrupted the work of the entire vineyard with your ridiculous picture taking."

"Since my father is going to put you on the cover of *Renown* magazine, I didn't think you'd complain. Surely you do want pictures of your wine empire to appear in the pages of the most widely read, weekly news magazine in the country?" She put a perfectly manicured hand on his arm.

"Is this your father's idea or one of yours, Dianne?" He still sounded irritated.

"Darling, no one tells Foster Bennett what to put in his magazine." She patted his arm. "Not even me." She angled her head then, slanting her hazel eyes toward Gayle. "Ramon is lacking in manners at times," she said, with a musical laugh. "In fact, he's often that way after a long flight. He forgot to introduce us. I'm Dianne Bennett."

"Gayle Eberly . . ." Gayle hesitated, waiting to see if Ramon would explain her presence here at the winery or if she should. His taciturn attitude made her decide not to elaborate. If Ramon wanted his beautiful visitor to know why he had flown her to his vineyards, let him tell her himself.

Dianne appeared to give her only a cursory look, but Gayle was not fooled by her seemingly perfunctory examination. Those gold-flecked brown eyes had been sizing her up much as the coach of a rival team scouts the opposition.

"Ramon, is Gayle here to take a tour of the winery?" Dianne made her question sound innocent enough, but it was apparent she was keenly curious as to why Ramon had brought another girl to his vineyards.

"Not this afternoon, it's too late. Anyway, there's plenty of time for it later as Gayle will be here in Bahía Kino for a while." He moved his arm, causing Dianne to remove her hand. Gayle wondered if Ramon were not deliberately being obscure to annoy Dianne. There certainly did seem to be strong emotional undercurrents between these two, which were making Gayle feel like an uncomfortable bystander.

Fortunately, at that moment a maroon sports car pulled up in front of the iron gates. "Good, there's Fernando to drive us to Casa del Mar." Ramon put his hand under Gayle's elbow, guiding her toward the waiting car.

"Wait, Ramon." The silky smoothness was gone from Dianne Bennett's voice as she took two steps to follow after them. "I did not come all the way from New York only to take pictures, Ramon. I came down here to see you."

Ramon turned back at her words. "That's a switch—New York to Bahía Kino. But then, I'm sure you have a round trip ticket." The look he gave her matched the coolness of his voice.

"I rented a car in Hermosillo to drive down from the airport," she said, calmly ignoring his cryptic words. "If you'll stay with me now, so we can talk, I'll drive you into town later."

"Now *you* are asking *me* to stay?" He ran a hand through his thick black hair, his eyes scrutinizing her alluring face. "That's a new role for you to play, Dianne, and, I must admit, surprisingly out of character." He shrugged. "But—all right." Turning back to Gayle, he took hold of her arm and led her across the plaza to where Fernando stood, holding the car door open for her.

"Drive Señorita Eberly to Casa del Mar, Fernando," he addressed the Mexican. "I'll come later."

"*Sí.*" The older man nodded.

"Maria will help you unpack and see that you are settled comfortably," Ramon said to Gayle, helping her into the car. As soon as he closed the door after her, he spun around and walked back to where Dianne stood waiting for him. Gayle could picture the look of triumph shimmering in those hazel eyes as she watched the tall Mexican walk away from the car and back across the plaza to her.

Abruptly, Gayle yanked her dark glasses from her face and rubbed her hand across her eyes. She didn't want to continue seeing the other girl's face in her mind, and though it should not be any concern of hers, she knew she resented Dianne's proprietary manner regarding Ramon. The two of them were well acquainted, that much was obvious. And though he had been angry when he discovered she was there at the vineyards, disrupting things with her picture taking, she had managed to convince him readily enough to stay there with her. Was this strikingly beautiful girl from New York the all important woman in Ramon's life? Or did he view her as he did other American women, as frivolous? If so, he seemed willing enough to tolerate her presence, and Gayle would bet that the fact that she was Foster Bennett's daughter could be the deciding factor. From what she had seen so far of the arrogant vintner, he would relish the prospect of being covered by the press, and *Renown* was not only widely circulated in the United States, but was translated into various foreign languages, as well. No, Ramon Albariza could hardly resist an offer of such publicity. Not unlike Ken, she thought with a shiver of distaste, which caused a frown to tighten the corners of her eyes. It appeared that a girl with an influential father had no difficulty in acquiring the attention of the man she wanted.

Pulling at the corner of her lip with her teeth, she wondered why she was allowing herself to get worked up over whose daughter Ramon chose to spend his time with. It mattered not at all to her, for he meant nothing in her life. He was her employer and that was all. Just a willful, arrogant man from whom she wished to learn winemaking and nothing else. Meanwhile, Ramon Albariza could pursue or be pursued by Dianne Bennett or any other woman and it did not concern her in the slightest. She laughed, hoping Dianne Bennett was as conniving as she appeared. It would serve him right. She laughed again.

"*Qué?* What is it, *señorita?*" Fernando angled his head at her.

"Nothing," she answered his questioning look. "I

thought of something amusing and I guess I laughed aloud, Mr. Montoya."

"Fernando," he corrected her. "I would like it if you called me Fernando. I am Maria's husband and we'll see much of each other, both at the *casa* and the vineyards."

She smiled her agreement and thought she was surely going to like this good-natured Mexican. His easy, relaxed manner made her feel more comfortable than she had at any other time today. Though she had heard him say little, when he had spoken, the deep, rich timbre of his voice made her think that he probably was a vibrant baritone. He seemed the type of man who might sing bright and happy Spanish songs as he worked in the vineyard unless, of course, the mirthless Señor Albariza didn't allow such displays. "I will not tolerate any disruptive element in my vineyard"—she grimaced, recalling Ramon's words to her after they had left the customs office in Hermosillo. Her musings were interrupted by Fernando honking the horn, then veering the car sharply in order to avoid a collision with a farm truck piled high with melons. The battered vehicle was chugging down the center of the narrow highway, its scratched and dented metal body vibrating as it went.

Gayle braced herself, pushing her hands against the dashboard. "That driver must be drunk. He's driving in the very middle of the road," she said, sucking in her breath in a frightened gasp.

"It's usually that way here." He shrugged. "I guess the road is smoother down the center." She found his casual acceptance unbelievable when they had so narrowly escaped an accident.

"But the highway is only two lanes and very

70

narrow! There aren't even any shoulders to give you room enough to pull off safely."

He shrugged again. "You'll discover many of our highways in Mexico are this way. One learns to accept it." His good-natured laugh did not dispel her anxieties.

"I'd be afraid to drive a car here."

"Don't worry, you won't have to. You leave the driving to Ramon or to me. It's better that Americans do not drive here, for even a minor accident makes serious problems," he said, resuming speed now that there were, for the moment, no other vehicles in sight. "Many a tourist from the United States has had to spend several uncomfortable days in one of our altogether unpleasant jails, for the traffic laws here are prejudiced in favor of our own people." A mischievous glint sparked in his dark brown eyes. "The Señorita Bennett had an accident the last time she was here and had to stay five hours in the jail at Hermosillo before Ramon went up to arrange for her release." Fernando's solemn tone was at variance with his amused expression. It seemed apparent to Gayle that the jovial Mexican had small regard for the sophisticated Dianne. She frowned, wondering if, like Ramon, Fernando thought of her as shallow, too. She hoped not, and she hoped, too, that she could prove herself to be an able worker at the winery.

The road now began a wide sweeping curve as it wound around a high plateau with a flat top and steep, rocky sides. As the car completed the curve, Gayle held her breath in awe, for now she caught her first glimpse of the ocean. The water was sapphire blue and sparkled like a fabulous jewel under the low afternoon sun. The azure sky reached down to meet the sea, the lighter shade a striking contrast to the deep rich color of the water. The road straightened and ran along beside the sandy beach. Gayle followed the shoreline, her eyes intent on the incredible beauty of the famed Sea of Cortez. Three large birds appeared, flying in a line as if following a leader. One at a time, she watched them dip down to the water and swoop up fish in the pouch which hung from their lower bill.

"Aren't those pelicans?" she asked, pointing.

Fernando turned his head to look. "Our name for them is *alcatraz*, but you call them pelicans—that's right. You'll see many here, and they are friendly birds; often one will settle down on the beach quite close to me when I'm fishing." He slowed the car and directed her attention toward a tree-covered island a short distance offshore. "That island is called Alcatraz because the pelicans build their nests there. It's a quiet, uninhabited place, except for the birds, that is."

"Can people go there?"

"Oh yes. In fact, the Señora Louise used to go often, and enjoyed spending hours there. Ramon's father built a shelter, a small *cabaña*, for her."

"I'd love to see it." Her voice lifted with excitement. "Do you think I could ask Ramon to take me?"

Fernando hesitated, his expression sobering. "Carmelita goes to the island to sketch. I'll ask her to take you."

She inclined her head. "Who's Carmelita?"

"My daughter," he answered, his full face expanding as a grin curved his fleshy cheeks and wiped away the solemnity. "At least, to Maria and me she is like our own. We adopted her when she was a few weeks

72

old." He scratched his chin thoughtfully. "I will have her take you next time she goes, if you like," he said, returning to the subject of the island. "That would be best, for Ramon has not gone back to Alcatraz since the plane crash."

Gayle gave Fernando a startled look. "Ramon crashed his plane?" Her face paled. "But, he—he said—why, he assured me that he had flown for many years. I—I assumed he had never crashed—" The words stuck in her dry throat.

"No, no, *señorita*. I didn't mean Ramon," the Mexican interrupted. "It was Señor Arnoldo and Señora Louise." His forehead shone with perspiration and he hunched his shoulders, at the same time shaking his head in denial to her fears. "I thought you had been told." His usually happy voice now held the bleak note of sadness. "It was almost two years ago now, the *señor* was bringing Ramon's mother back from Mexico City. We think he misjudged the island in the darkness of the night, thinking it was the vineyard. Who knows?" Fernando continued to shake his head slowly. "The small plane went into the sea; it was a terrible tragedy." His face was drawn, and somehow she knew this was a subject he would never have mentioned if he had known she knew nothing about it. She was curious about Ramon's mother, especially so because of the reference Ramon had made to her on the plane today. While she was wondering how she might subtly pursue the subject with Fernando, she realized he was slowing the car as they approached a low, ivory-colored stucco wall covered by cascading blossoms of vivid purple bougainvillaea.

"This is Casa del Mar," Fernando said, pulling the

73

car off the road into a driveway at one side of the house, where he parked under a portico.

Looking at the wall which enclosed the Spanish-style house on three sides, she realized that the front of the house was toward the wide sandy beach and thus faced the jewel-toned water of the ocean. Casa del Mar, "House of the Ocean," was aptly named. Leaving the car, she and Fernando walked through a garden courtyard at the back of the *casa*. It was a rectangular area planted with pink and white olean-der, yellow marigolds, and vivid, flame-colored pop-pies and the mixture of multicolored flowers lent a light, spicy fragrance to the warm air.

Entering through the back door, Gayle found herself in a large, sunny kitchen, the walls of which were festooned with strings of dried red peppers, and on the wide windowsills gaudily painted clay pots were filled with chives and assorted other herbs which gave off a pungent, earthy smell. In one corner of the large room there was a recessed space which held a wine rack filled with at least three dozen bottles of wine, each bottle placed horizon-tally in its separate slot. Gayle found the attract-ive kitchen as picturesque as a travel poster.

"Maria is probably upstairs seeing about your room." Pushing open a swinging door as he spoke, Fernando called out, "Maria! Maria, the Señorita Eberly is here." Holding the door wide so Gayle could pass through, he added, "Maria will be right along. I'll get your luggage from the car."

She walked down the hall, which led through a wide archway into a spacious room with a high-beamed ceiling. Two stairways, one at each side of the vast living room, rose to meet a beautiful railed balcony which ran along the second story. As she moved to the center of the room, she was struck by the magenta tile floor, for it had a waxed sheen which added to the intriguing beauty of the intricately patterned tiles. While the perimeters of the floor were bare of covering, the center area of the room was covered by a deep pile rug the color of rich cream, bordered with a wide band of aquamarine. The low couches and numerous upholstered chairs which furnished the area harmonized with the rug, being covered either in the turquoise of the border or the deep ivory of the center.

Scarcely had she sat down on one of the couches when she heard quick footsteps moving along the balcony above, and then a small, slim woman glided down the stairs at one end of the room. As she hurried forward to greet Gayle, her compact face relaxed in a smile in such a way that Gayle thought of the tight petals of a rosebud opening to form a perfect flower. It was as if the Mexican woman had looked at Gayle first with surprise and then with warm acceptance.

"You're Maria, of course," Gayle said, returning the housekeeper's smile. Looking at Maria, she estimated her age at near fifty and guessed she was at least five years younger than Fernando. Her olive skin was free of wrinkles except for the etched creases at the corners of her deep-set brown eyes, and though she was smiling, Gayle thought there was a hint of sadness mirrored in the dark pools of her eyes.

"I apologize for not being downstairs to meet you." She looked at Gayle for another long moment before lowering her head and running both hands over her skirt and apron, as if she were making certain her appearance was neat. "But my husband, he drives so fast," she chuckled. "I didn't expect you to arrive from the vineyard for another quarter of an hour."

Gayle nodded in agreement. "I discovered just now that everyone drives fast in Mexico, but fortunately, your husband is skilled and he doesn't drive in the middle of the highway as everyone else seems to do."

At that moment, Fernando entered the room with her suitcases. "I'll take these on up to the guest room," he said, and started across the room to the far staircase.

"No, Fernando," Maria's shoulders stiffened and her voice was decisive. "Take the *señorita*'s things to the blue room."

He turned back, a puzzled look on his round face. "But—Maria, you know—"

"I know she will enjoy the blue room," she interrupted him, and her firm tone clearly indicated that she would tolerate no arguments from her husband. "Besides, you said Señorita Bennett was at the vineyards. If she's staying *she* will use the guest room."

Fernando's brows lowered over questioning eyes, but with the characteristic shrug which seemed part of his accepting attitude, he recrossed the room and started up the other stairway. He moved briskly, and before Gayle and Maria had ascended halfway, Fernando had already deposited her luggage in the room, crossed the balcony to the other side and was coming down the opposite staircase. Whether he had done this to escape further orders from his wife or merely to get out of their way, she did not know. Certainly the graceful stairs were wide enough to allow three people to pass with ease; in fact, Gayle was discovering that every area of Casa del Mar had been designed to a spacious scale.

Reaching the upper level, Maria stepped aside to allow Gayle to precede her into the bedroom. Entering, Gayle felt that this had to be the loveliest and most inviting room she had ever seen. From floor to ceiling, the long rectangular chamber was decorated in shades of blue with accents of lavendar and white. The walls made her think of a morning sky traced with white clouds, for the color was the palest blue, with a delicate, almost fragile, quality about it. The carpet was of a deeper shade, a French blue reminiscent of Sèvres porcelain. Sheer white curtains hung at the casement windows and covered the double French doors at one end of the room. The quilted satin spread which covered the wide bed was designed with sprays of blue and lavender flowers which looked like cameos on the white silken background, and on a low table next to the bed, an exquisite amethyst glass lamp bore a white silk shade pleated in dozens of tiny folds. Every aspect of this pastel-colored room would have complemented the blond beauty of Ramon's mother, and without being told, Gayle knew that this had been the Señora Louise's room and reflected her discerning taste.

"What a gorgeous room this is. And blue is my favorite color. I know I'll love staying here." She moved around the room, admiring the rich patina of the antique highboy and the smooth wax finish of the gleaming mahogany writing desk.

"*Sí, sí.*" Maria's face glowed. "I knew you would enjoy this room, *señorita*. And, too, I think perhaps you will like going to sleep to the sound of the sea." She moved silently across the thick carpet and opened the French doors to reveal the wide balcony

that ran along the front of the *casa* and afforded a
magnificent view of the sloping white sandy beach
and the ocean, which now, in the fading sunlight,
had changed in color from sapphire blue to a vibrant
emerald green. Gayle had followed the petite Mexican woman and now she walked the width of the
balcony and, leaning her arms on the wrought-iron
balustrade, she gazed out at the sea. The tide was
going out now, and the waves, washing against the
shore, had a soporific effect. She took a deep breath,
smelling the sharpness of salt in the air. The pelicans, as well as several large white gulls, were flying
low over the water. Suddenly, a porpoise leaped
clear of the water, his glistening body curved in an
arc above the green surface of the sea, and she
smiled delightedly. She had no idea how long she
remained standing there, but when she turned back
to the room, she discovered Maria had gone. But
not, however, before she had placed the larger of
Gayle's suitcases on a luggage rack near the closet.
Gayle sighed softly, grateful for the housekeeper's
helpfulness. What was it Ramon had said about
Maria? That she would pamper her as she had his
mother? Ramon himself seemed both critical and
even scornful of his mother. What an enigmatic man
he was. She was filled with curiosity about him.
Maybe he said he didn't admire American females,
but his actions belied his words. Dianne Bennett's
possessive claims on him certainly stemmed from
some prior relationship, didn't they? And if he *had*
been involved with her—was he still?

She pushed aside these questions and began to
unpack. In less than half an hour she had her clothes
hanging in the huge closet and everything else neatly
placed in two of the deep drawers of the highboy.

She chose the drawers in the middle of the tall chest as the two bottom drawers she discovered were being used for storage. It had grown late, and outside the daylight had faded, leaving the room filled with murky shadows. She pressed the light switch and discovered that it controlled a pair of wall sconces behind the bed. These now spread their soft radiance throughout the room.

Glancing at her watch, she was surprised to find it was almost seven. She wondered if Ramon had returned from the vineyards, and if he hadn't, whether he would come soon. Having had only a sandwich and coffee since breakfast, she was starved, and she was looking forward to her first meal prepared in Casa del Mar. While she was washing in the blue and white bathroom which adjoined her bedroom she noticed that the spacious tiled bath must also serve another bedroom, as there was a second door which stood partly ajar.

Peering into the burgundy-carpeted room beyond, she saw that a massive bed and two heavy chests of drawers, all of dark-grained rosewood, lined the parchment white walls. Whose room was it? Surely such masculine furniture would not be in the guest room Maria had indicated Dianne Bennett might use. Gayle quietly pulled the door to the other bedroom closed, still wondering whose it was.

Returning to stand before the mirror, she snatched up her lipstick and splashed bright color across her lips. Why should it matter to her whether the adjoining room was the guest room or not? Or, for that matter, whether the stunning New Yorker was to be a guest at Casa del Mar or not? She glared at her own image in the mirror. Fatigue pinched the corners of her eyes, dimming their usual luster. How tired she was, but then, it had been a long day, and, in so many ways, a curious one. Rubbing her bottom lip with the tip of her little finger, she smoothed color along the contours of her mouth. Without wanting to, she recalled those few minutes when Ramon's lips had taken such exciting possession of hers. Snatching up a tissue, she wiped the excess lipstick from her finger with a savage gesture and hurried out of the bathroom. As soon as she flicked off the wall sconces she left her bedroom, and as she started downstairs she heard the chiming of a clock. It was a quarter past seven, so surely Ramon would have come back for dinner by now, she thought, as she continued down the stairs.

Two tall lamps had been turned on in the living room, but there was no one in sight. The high-ceilinged room was silent and empty, and if anything, it seemed even larger that it had appeared earlier. She hunched her shoulders nervously, rubbing her hand across the back of her neck. It gave her a strange feeling to be alone in this place, for lovely as the house was, its owner lacked its warmth, and this made her distinctly uncomfortable. Not wanting to stay in the living room by herself, she walked the length of the room and started down the hall to the kitchen.

Chapter Five

"Papa said Dianne Bennett had been at the vineyard since noon. How dare she come back here?" Gayle could hear a girl's angry voice as she approached the doorway to the kitchen. "Surely Ramon isn't planning to bring her back to Casa del Mar?"

"I have not been told, Carmelita, but if he does, you watch your tongue," Maria's quiet voice cautioned.

"Ramon is a fool if he has anything more to do with that shallow redhead." The girl's voice was laced with disgust.

"Hush now! I don't like to hear you speak with disrespect of Ramon." Gayle caught sight of Maria shaking a small paring knife, with which she was peeling peaches, at a young Mexican girl who was leaning against the kitchen wall next to the wine rack, one hand planted defiantly on her slender hip.

"Excuse me," Gayle said quickly, as she pushed the swinging door open further and entered the kitchen, "I finished unpacking and I—I wondered if Ramon had come home." She stammered as she spoke, feeling flustered at having overheard their conversation and not wanting to give the impression she had deliberately been eavesdropping.

Maria had been sitting at the counter preparing the peaches, now she hopped down from her tall stool and quickly wiped her juice-covered hands on a red- and white-striped dish towel. "Oh, Señorita Gayle, I'm glad you're well settled in your room and now I know you surely must be hungry. I'm preparing a nice dinner for you." Her words were gentle, motherly.

She *is* pampering me, just as Ramon said she would, Gayle thought, taking pleasure in the Mexican woman's concern for her.

The pretty girl with the dark flowing hair had been watching Gayle since she entered the room. Now she took several steps toward her, seeming to scrutinize her at closer range with large, smoke-colored eyes. "You're the American girl from the Napa Valley," she said, and smiled at Gayle. "Papa told me he'd driven you here from the vineyard and that you were pretty and I'd like you. Papa was right." She wrinkled her pert nose like a contented rabbit, her heart-shaped face guileless. "Do you think you'll like it here in Mexico?"

"Go set the table in the dining room, Carmelita," Maria interrupted sharply. "And don't bother Señorita Eberly with your silly questions."

"I—I do like it here already . . ." She hesitated, then continued, as she looked from Maria to her daughter. "Please, won't both of you call me Gayle? I'll be much more comfortable if you do."

Before she had finished speaking, a low whistle

sounded from outside in the courtyard. Carmelita spun around and gave Maria a pleading look. "It's Juan; I've got to go, Mama. Excuse me this time—about the table, I mean." Almost before the words were out of her mouth, the exuberant girl shot out of the kitchen with the speed of an arrow leaving a bow and disappeared into the dusky twilight of the courtyard.

A frown of irritation creased Maria's brow. "It will be a relief to have that girl settled in Monterrey at the university," she said with a shrug of her thin shoulders. "She's impetuous and, like Señor Ramon says, she must study to develop her talent. Carmelita is an artist." Maria said this last with pride in her voice.

"Fernando mentioned to me that your daughter did some sketching over on the small island. It's wonderful to be skilled that way; I know you're both proud of her." Gayle's voice held real sincerity, for she could readily see that this pretty girl was the center of Maria and Fernando's life. "This is her first year at college, isn't it?" she asked with polite interest.

"Sí, she is barely eighteen, and as you could see, she's a bold one, but the señor, he insisted on the university, and he is making it possible. Ramon is a kind and generous man, exactly as his father was." Maria spoke reverently, much as if she were speaking of a patron saint.

Gayle turned and walked to the window, pretending an interest in the herbs growing on the sill. She wanted to change the topic. When it came to Ramon Albariza, she, for one, did not recognize such benevolent characteristics as Maria obviously atttributed to him. Suppressing a smile, she thought that she found him to be far more an arrogant devil than a saint.

"Now, if you'll show me where the things are, I'll set the table." She turned back to Maria and extended her hands. "Since I'm to be here for six months, you mustn't wait on me and treat me as a guest."

"You may help later on, but not on your first night here." Maria removed a pitcher of ice water from the refrigerator as she spoke. "There are certain traditions at Casa del Mar for the welcoming of a new guest." Maria's round eyes shone like a pair of jet black buttons and Gayle got the definite impression that the traditions of the *casa* were important and not to be altered.

"How soon do you expect Ramon for dinner, then?" she questioned, moving over to stand by the wine rack, out of Maria's way while she bustled around, taking silverware from a drawer and china from a shelf of one of the wall cupboards.

"No, *señorita*." She shook her dark head briskly. "The *señor* is not coming. He called to say he would not be able to get here for dinner, but I have something good prepared for you. I'll serve you in half an hour." She took a tall-stemmed goblet and filled it with water from the pitcher as she spoke.

Anger mixed with disappointment in Gayle's mind; he certainly was making it clear how little her comfort meant to him, she thought. She spun around, wanting to hide her feelings from the older woman. "Please call me when you want me to come for dinner," she said, starting to leave the kitchen. "I'll go out on the porch where I can watch the waves and hear the sea."

Not waiting to see if Maria had anything more to

say, Gayle left the kitchen and charged through the living room to the porch. She seethed with anger, all of it directed toward the absent Ramon. What a rude man he was. How could he be so insensitive? Didn't he realize how embarrassing it was for her to be a guest in a house without a host? It had been awkward enough to be left to the care of Fernando at the vineyards, then thrust into the *casa* to impose on his housekeeper, without this added humiliation. At the very least he could have arranged to have dinner with her. It was, after all, *his* plan that she should live in his home during her months in Mexico. She clenched her teeth, thinking of his total indifference to her feelings. He obviously was not quite so indifferent to the svelte Dianne. Further irritation caused a wave of heat to bathe her face and throat. She lifted her hair off the back of her neck so the air could reach her skin. Though the intense heat of the day had lessened with the sunset, the breeze was still quite warm. She fanned her face with her free hand.

"*Por favor.*" Maria's soothing voice announced her presence in the doorway and she approached, carrying a small silver tray on which was a single cut crystal wine glass. "*Por favor,*" she said again, "please, I have a glass of the Albariza sherry from the Spanish vineyards for you. At Casa del Mar, it is offered in welcome. Señor Ramon, when he called, reminded me you must be served his grandfather's sherry on this, your first night in Bahía Kino.

After what had happened, she found it difficult to believe Ramon had given a single thought to making her feel welcome in his house, but she did feel grateful to Maria for attempting to make the evening as pleasant as possible under the circumstances.

"Thank you." She forced herself to smile, hoping

the resentment she held for Ramon would not be communicated to the kind-hearted woman. "I'm pleased." She took the glass from the tray and held it carefully in her hand. After admiring the color of the wine for a moment, she bent her head slightly to smell its bouquet. Feeling Maria's eyes on her, she realized the other woman was waiting for her reaction. Carefully, Gayle took a sip of the amber wine and rolled it across her tongue. It was a trifle sweeter than she had anticipated. She hesitated a fraction of a second, then tasted it a second time. Glancing up, she caught the expectant look in the Mexican woman's sparkling eyes.

"It's excellent." Gayle's voice rang with assurance. "I've never had a finer sherry. The taste is exactly what my father told me to look for in a good sherry; Spanish *amontillado* always has a kind of nutty taste."

Maria beamed. "Your father has taught you well," she declared, her eyes glistening as she added, "Señor Ramon will someday soon produce a golden wine as fine as his grandfather's, and he'll do it using his own Mexican grapes." She nodded her head in emphasis. "He has a great wish to accomplish this, and my Fernando says that each year the grapes here improve, and soon they will equal the grapes of Jerez de la Frontera, in Spain." She paused, as if afraid she might be talking too much.

"That's the sherry zone, the famous wine country of Spain, isn't it?" Gayle reassured her with a smile.

"*Sí, sí*—and I was there once. Señor Arnoldo and the Señora Louise, they took me with them to care for little Ramon. He was only four years old at the time."

"I've never been to Spain, and I'd love to go. How

exciting it must have been for you." Gayle was intrigued, and she wanted Maria to go on talking. She hadn't imagined that Maria had been with the family for so long. If she had known Ramon since he was a small child, she must have come to work for Ramon's mother when she was no older than Carmelita was now. "Tell me about the trip, Maria, please."

"Ramon's grandfather had been ill and dying, and Señor Arnoldo felt the old gentleman should see his only grandson before he died. It was a sad but memorable trip." A melancholy note entered her voice. "It was the only time the three generations of Albariza men were to be together in the same place."

"Then you were there when the old Señor Albariza died?"

She nodded. "It was at the old man's funeral that I learned how the family got the name. They took it from the grape producing area in the province of Cadiz."

"What do you mean?" She squinted her eyes, perplexed by Maria's curious statement.

Maria straightened importantly, noticeably pleased to have aroused such interest. "*Albariza* is the Spanish name given to the hard, chalky soil which contains a lot of lime. Grapes grown in this soil produce the *fino* sherries, the finest," she stated proudly. "This is a well-known fact in Spain."

"I don't doubt you." Gayle shook her head. "But I don't understand about the family name being the same as that of the soil."

"You will have to ask Señor Ramon how true the story is, but Señora Louise told me that it happened many, many years ago. They say a peasant boy, a poor youth with no family and no name, labored in the vineyards in Marcharnudo, near Jerez. He was bold and a hard worker, and in time he had vineyards of his own which, of course, he passed on to his sons. He called himself merely Pedro in the beginning, but when he became a man of property he took the name of the soil of his vineyards and became known as Pedro Carlos de Albariza. This Pedro was Ramon's great-great-grandfather." Maria's face held a rapt expression; she seemed totally engrossed in the story she was telling. "Many years later, when Ramon's father left Spain to come to Mexico to start the Albariza vineyards here, he was called Don Arnoldo de Albariza. In Mexico, however, it sounded too European and he soon simplified his name to Arnoldo Albariza. Then, when Ramon was born, he was christened Ramon Santos Albariza."

"It's like a marvelous, romantic legend," Gayle sighed, fascinated at hearing this picturesque story of Ramon's heritage. "Thank you for telling me. Now I will enjoy the sherry of Ramon's grandfather even more." Gayle sensed that this thoughtful woman had told her the family story in an effort to make her feel more comfortable here at Casa del Mar, which was something Ramon had certainly made little effort to do. The thought of her absent host filled her with renewed irritation.

By the time she had finished dinner it had grown dark outside, and the crescent moon seemed far away, out over the sea. What pale light it did offer appeared to be absorbed by the ocean before it could reach the shore. The August night air was extremely warm and it smelled of seaweed and salt water. The lapping waves, rolling in to the shore and then slowly retreating, made a rhythmic sound which made Gayle think of a Spanish dancer swaying gracefully to the gradually slowing beat of her castanets. As she lay in the comfortable bed, she welcomed these pleasant sounds, hoping they would lull her to sleep, for she wished somehow to fill her mind with something other than the aggravation she felt toward Ramon Albariza.

Had she slept? She must have, but she was awake now, and she felt very warm, her body was moist with perspiration. It must have been the lack of air stirring in the room that had caused her to wake up. She rubbed her hand across her forehead, discovering that her face felt damp and somewhat feverish. Sitting up, she wondered what time it was, but she didn't want to know badly enough to turn on the light and add even a breath more heat to the room. What breeze there had been when she went to bed had surely died away, or changed direction and blown out to sea, for the air now encased her like a smothering cocoon.

She got up and, crossing the length of the room in her bare feet, she went out on the balcony. Blessedly, it was a little cooler outside. She stretched her arms over her head, turning slowly. The moon, which seemed to have moved closer into shore, now spilled silver light onto the corner of the balcony where she stood.

"You found it too hot to sleep?"

Gayle let out a startled exclamation at the sound of Ramon's low voice. Whirling around, she stared across the balcony, trying to locate him in the darkness. All she could see was the small red ember of a cigarette, glowing in the blackness at the other end of the balcony. "I—I had no idea anyone was out here. Where—where are you, anyway? I—I can't see you," she stammered in her embarrassment.

"Well, I can see you. And I must admit, you're a beautiful sight with that shapely body of yours covered in moonlight and very little else." His words were accompanied by a low, sensual laugh.

Flinging her arms across her breasts, she jumped quickly back into the dark corner of the balcony next to her bedroom. "Stay where you are," she said angrily. "Don't you dare come anywhere near me." Her voice shook, but she hoped that he had failed to notice this sign that his presence upset her.

"That's why I'm out here in the first place, just to keep from alarming your shy, maidenly senses." He laughed again.

"What do you mean?"

"I mean my bedroom adjoins yours. I knew if you heard me in the bathroom between our two rooms, you'd make a worse scene than you did at finding me in your precious vineyard back home." The ember glowed deeper in the darkness and she caught a whiff of the aromatic tobacco of the slender brown cigarrillo.

So the burgundy carpeted room was Ramon's. The discovery didn't really surprise her, for the bold, masculine appearance of that bedroom certainly fit the image she had of him.

"I don't know what you're doing in the blue room in the first place." A note of anger and annoyance was now discernible in his voice. "The guest room is in the other wing of the *casa* and you'd have been undisturbed there, as well as a good deal cooler. That room has a ceiling fan."

"I'm here because your housekeeper gave me this room," she countered defiantly. "I think she had the idea that your friend Dianne would be using the guest room."

"Where did she get that foolish idea?" he snapped.

"How should I know? Since this is *your* house, if you didn't want me to have this particular room, you should have taken the time to inform your housekeeper of your wishes in the matter." She hurled the words out as fast as she could utter them. "Obviously, you were too involved elsewhere to bother."

"Ah ha, so that's it," he chuckled.

"That's what?"

"You're angry about my staying at the vineyard with Dianne."

"I don't care where you are or with whom." She let her tone show the extent of the contempt she felt. "What I *do* care about is that you put me in an enormously awkward situation. You thrust me on Fernando and Maria. They did what they could to make me comfortable in your absence, but you could have shown the good manners to act as host in your own home, not leave it to others."

"My, my, aren't you the outraged little miss. I take it from that barrage of words that you expect me to dance attendance on you for the duration of your stay here in my country?" He slurred his words in that maddening manner of his, and with every silky inflection of his accented voice Gayle became more incensed.

"I expect minimal courtesy, that's all. Couldn't you behave as a host on my first night in your house and show enough consideration to at least make it back for dinner?" she lashed out at him angrily.

"Wasn't your dinner satisfactory?" he asked with icy civility.

"It was delicious—of course, but that's hardly the point."

"And were you not served wine from the Albariza vineyards in Spain? The finest sherry in all the world?"

Though she couldn't see his face in the dark, she knew that a mocking smile must be curling his lips. He was belittling her and enjoying every minute of it.

"I didn't hear your answer, Gayle. You were served Albariza sherry, were you not?"

"You know very well I was," she hissed through clenched teeth.

"Then it would seem I am not totally the ill-mannered host."

She heard the scrape of metal against tile as he evidently pushed his chair back and stood up. She could just barely make out his tall, dark form moving to the railing of the balcony. The small red ember of his cigarette disappeared as he ground it out in a nearby sand-filled ashtray. "Since you feel I was remiss earlier in not seeing to your needs at Casa del Mar, I shall remedy the situation now." He crossed the balcony as he spoke, and she could hear the soft whisper of his bare feet against the tile as he moved toward her.

Suddenly, she sensed as much as saw his dark outline towering above her. Ramon was so close now that his warm breath fanned the damp tendrils of hair on her forehead. Too aware of his nearness, she took a step back. "It's a bit late to be concerned about your duties as host tonight," she said nervously, sensing that he had moved between her and the door to the bedroom. "If you'll excuse me, I—I'll say good—good night," she stammered.

"Let me assist you." He swept her up in his arms.

Momentarily speechless at his sudden action, her hands flew up as if to ward off danger. She felt the crisp hairs of his chest curling under her fingers. "You—you're undressed!"

"Only partially," he drawled. "I'm still wearing my trousers, although what you're wearing feels like nothing more than a cobweb."

"Put me down!" She felt panic rising inside her.

"In a minute," he said, unperturbed, and, striding through the open French doors, he brushed the light switch with his elbow. The wall sconces glowed softly and she stared up into the chiseled features of the face so near her own. He was looking at her, his head tilted and a devilish glint in his eyes.

Alarmed, she was aware that beneath the thin lace of her gown her breasts were rising and falling with the effort of her breathing. She knew Ramon was aware of it, too, for his eyes clung to the curving contours.

"Put me down—this instant," she gasped. Frantically, she kicked her legs and at the same time began to pound her fists against the muscled hardness of his chest. "What do you think you're doing?" Her voice rose shrilly in the midnight stillness of the room.

"I'm acting the thoughtful host, as you requested. I'm escorting my guest to her bed." One corner of his mouth curled with wry humor.

How dare he laugh at her? He was the most obnoxious man she'd ever met. "I didn't request anything of the sort." The quiver in her voice revealed how apprehensive she was. "Let me go!"

A wicked grin revealed his even white teeth. "Ask

me politely and I might," he teased, pulling her closer. He tightened his arms, effectively immobilizing her so she could no longer move her hands against his chest. With deliberate slowness, he lowered his dark head to brush his lips along the soft curve of her cheek, then nibbled the lobe of her ear. She felt breathless, as if she was about to faint.

"*Querida*," he murmured huskily, "you smell like the honey-filled flowers of Andalusia."

"It's—it's only cologne—" she stammered inanely. "I put it on to make me feel cool."

"And do you feel cool?" The question mocked her. He was kissing her neck now, his warm lips sending heat pulsing through her veins.

Stifling a moan of pleasure at the delicious sensations he was arousing in her, she pressed her lips tightly together as if to hold back her treacherous emotions. "You—you can put me down now," she said in a low voice.

He lifted his head and looked into her eyes, his expression unreadable. Then, taking his time, he walked over to the bed and deposited her unceremoniously on the rumpled blue sheets. His dark eyes mocked her. "As you like, but you *had* asked me to show some personal attention to my guest. Don't you find my hospitality pleasing?"

"No. I find your actions distasteful beyond words."

"Distasteful, eh?" One eyebrow rose. "I got the impression you enjoyed it. After all, isn't it what you wanted?"

"You know it's not! Now get out of my room and leave me alone." Her voice was strangled now with angry tears.

"But you were complaining that I had left you

alone all evening. Really, my lovely Gayle, it seems to me you're rather confused about exactly what it is you do want of me." His voice was slurred and honeyed and his dark eyes sparked with barely suppressed laughter.

Cold fury marked her own eyes. "Stop making fun of me. You've made your point, Ramon. Now have the decency to go to your own room and let me be. I think now that it will be best if we have nothing to do with each other outside of the winery."

"And just how do you suggest we accomplish that feat?" His lips curled without humor.

"You can ignore my presence in your house. After all, I'm only a silly, frivolous American female." She threw his words back at him with undisguised sarcasm.

"Frivolous maybe, but difficult to ignore when you wear that film of green mist and appear bathed in moonlight on my balcony."

"Well, I told you I wanted to find some other place to stay," she flared.

"And *I* told *you*—there is no other place suitable for an American girl to stay in Bahía Kino," he said grimly.

She saw the stubborn hardness of his jaw. "Let's not argue, Ramon," she said tiredly. "I'm hot and tired and if I don't get some sleep soon I won't be alert enough to start work at the vineyards tomorrow."

He didn't comment, but his eyes locked with hers for a long moment. Turning slowly, he walked across to the rosewood highboy. Opening the bottom drawer, he sorted through the contents, then pulled out a folded article of white cloth. Returning to the bed he handed the gauzelike fabric to Gayle. "Here, put this on. It's a summer gown of my mother's and made of cotton, which you'll find a great deal better suited to our climate than that scrap of sophisticated finery you're wearing. You can be more comfortable here if you adopt our ways." He stressed his words meaningfully. "And, in fact, if you want to know what I think, the way you're shaped you'll make even this cotton shift seem sexy."

"I don't care what you think." She glared at him.

"Oh, don't you now? I think you care a good deal more than you want to admit." He stood beside the bed, looking down at her, his dark lashes screening his eyes. "I'll get an electric fan from my room for you, but put this on before I get back," he ordered, as if speaking to a recalcitrant child.

He had been issuing commands since the moment they'd met and she'd had more than enough of it. "I'll change when you've gone away to stay away, and not before," she said defiantly.

"Either you put the shift on while I get the fan," he said flatly, "or when I get back, I'll do it for you." He strode off toward his own room.

Still churning with indignation, Gayle pulled the green nylon over her head with frantic haste. Yanking the white gown down over her shoulders, she smoothed the cool cotton fabric over her hot flesh. She would have enjoyed defying Ramon's orders, but she didn't doubt for one minute that he had every intention of carrying out his threat. The loose shift was cut almost to the waist in front, exposing the valley between her firm, round breasts. Springing from the bed, she ran to the dresser to seek a safety pin to fasten the neckline. She heard the door open from Ramon's room into the bathroom, so she abandoned her search, leaping back into bed.

Barely glancing toward where Gayle sat with the sheet clutched to her throat, Ramon positioned the fan on the floor in front of the window, angling the flow of air toward her. She heard the soft whirring sound of the circling blades and felt the pleasant breeze.

"How does that feel?" He took a couple of steps toward her. "Does that air blow over you?" He put his hand out to determine the airflow.

She felt herself tensing. "It's fine, it's perfect," she added quickly, not wanting him to come any closer. "Thank you."

"Are you certain you'll be comfortable now?"

Was he still mocking her? She couldn't tell. "I—I'm quite sure I can go right to sleep," she said, nodding her head nervously.

He made no move to come closer or to leave the room. He seemed to be studying her face. "Did you put on the cotton gown?"

"You told me to, didn't you?"

"Let me see," he said, coming another step nearer.

She shrank back against the pillows and lowered the sheet barely enough for him to see her shoulders.

He let his eyes flick over her. "Good," he said perfunctorily.

She forced herself to meet his gaze. "I'm sure I can sleep now, if you'll just switch off the lights as you leave."

Shrugging, he sauntered to the door and extinguished the lights. It took a second for her eyes to get accustomed to the darkness and then she could see Ramon's shadowy figure in the pale shaft of moonlight which came through the French doors to fall across the length of the room. He lounged in the doorway, one hand braced nonchalantly against the door frame.

"Oh, there is just one more thing . . ." He drew his words out slowly in that soft, slurring way of his, at the same time stepping back into the room.

"What—what do you think you're going to do now?" Her throat tightened and slivers of apprehension alerted all her senses. She felt like the defenseless deer facing the wolf.

"I'm going to kiss you good night, of course. You did criticize my lack of manners earlier this evening. I wish to make amends."

For a brief moment she felt a wanton desire for him to do just that. Appalled at her reaction to the insinuating softness of his words, she hugged the sheet against her breasts. Realizing he had started toward the bed, she gasped and blurted, "No! No! Don't come any closer!" She felt he must surely hear the pounding of her heart, for it sounded thunderous in her own ears.

"Another night, then," he said, soft laughter surrounding his words. "For I assure you, I intend to make certain that you experience the ultimate hospitality of Casa del Mar."

She could not see his expression in the dimness, but his voice filled her ears even after he left the room. She tried to get in a comfortable position for sleeping, wanting only to close her mind to the new and disturbing emotions that flooded over her. Why was she allowing herself to become personally involved with this compelling man? She must not forget the reason she came to Mexico in the first place. She was here to learn the art of winemaking, not to lose her head over the fascinating Ramon Albariza.

Chapter Six

Stretching her arms over her head, Gayle pulled herself from the fog of sleep, blinked her eyes, then widened them to discover that clear yellow sunlight was streaming in through the open French doors. Slowly, she brought her arms down, feeling the airy softness of the cotton shift. Recalling why she happened to be wearing it, she rubbed the material between her fingers and her lips formed a smile. Quickly, she slid across the blue sheets and, sliding her legs over the side of the bed, let her toes curl into the soft carpet. Still smiling, she thought it would seem that she was to be allowed to keep this lovely room for the duration of her stay at Casa del Mar, for there had been no sounds from Ramon's room either late last night, after he had left her, or this morning. Apparently he had moved to the other side of the house and was using the guest room with the

99

ceiling fan. She wrinkled her nose in delight at the idea and laughed at the thought of having won at least one round against the formidable Ramon Albariza.

She walked out onto the balcony, clutching the loose neck of the shift. The balcony railing was sufficiently high to shield her from the full view of anyone on the beach below. At the same time, she could lean over it and have an open vista of the ocean beyond. Gayle let out a sigh of pure pleasure, for the sea was calm and incredibly blue in the bright sunlight. The tide had gone out earlier, leaving the sand washed to a pearly whiteness and the air smelling faintly of kelp.

The pleasant rumble of the surf had obviously lured a pair of swimmers from their beds, for she caught sight of two glistening wet heads bobbing among the waves. She continued to watch them, and in a few minutes they reached the shore; a tall, bronzed man and a girl with long, dark hair falling around her bare shoulders and brushing across the brief top of her yellow bikini. Curiously, Gayle felt a prick of envy on realizing that the girl was Carmelita and the broad-shouldered man with the tapered torso of an athlete was Ramon.

As they ambled slowly toward the *casa,* the two of them were laughing and talking. When they got directly in front of the porch, they stopped, and stood facing each other, talking earnestly. At one point in their conversation, Carmelita flung her hair back from her face and gazed up at Ramon. Gayle could see how young and radiant she was and how beautiful, still touched with tiny drops of water that glistened like diamonds on her flawless skin. Gayle turned her head sharply so she wouldn't have to watch the two of them, for suddenly she was filled with resentment because of the easy rapport that they so evidently shared. Could she be jealous because Ramon seemed to care about the Mexican girl? She chewed the corner of her lip, ashamed of her ridiculous reaction to a scene which was, after all, none of her business. Stiffening her shoulders, she turned back to see Carmelita leaving Ramon and running toward the back of the *casa*.

Whether he had known before that she was on the balcony, or just happened now to glance up and see her at the railing, she did not know. But see her he did, and he lifted his hand and waved to her.

"You missed a great morning swim, Gayle." He stood with his feet apart, hands on his lean hips, looking up with a lazy smile spanning his handsome face. "I'd have awakened you, but after the restless night you'd had, I decided that, as a *thoughtful host,* I shouldn't bother you too early this morning." He allowed all that male charm of his to permeate his voice.

Before she could respond, he went on, "Get into your jeans and meet me for breakfast in fifteen minutes. You do start work at the vineyards this morning you know." He dropped his hand and strode out of sight beneath the balcony.

She gripped the railing so hard the iron bruised her palms. Why must he always be so high handed and bossy? She marched back into the bedroom and stepped out of the cotton shift. Frustration and anger surged through her. He had ordered her to wear this gown for sleeping and now he had determined that jeans were the uniform of the day. Well, after all, he had warned her. He had told her that everything in his *casa,* and in his vineyard, was

101

to be done his way—and so she either followed orders or she would have to give up and get out. She would never do that—she wouldn't give him that degree of satisfaction. Taking a pair of jeans and a blue shirt from the closet, she began to dress for her first day at Albariza Wines. Her lips curved in a smile of satisfaction as she fingered the white stitched pockets of her designer jeans. She would look exactly as she wanted to—trim, tailored and American—but still follow the letter of the law. She laughed out loud.

When Gayle arrived at the vineyards, after a quick and virtually silent breakfast with Ramon, Fernando met her and took her on a tour of several different areas in order for her to familiarize herself with the varieties of grapes that were grown in the region. She noted how developed the fruit was and how nearly fully ripened. She was not surprised, therefore, when Fernando informed her that the picking of the grapes would commence in ten days. His round face brightened with enthusiasm as he spoke of the harvest.

"Carmelita has never missed the wine fiesta and she has pestered Ramon and me to set the date early this year, ahead of the date she's due to enroll at the university." He grinned. "Thank goodness the weather has complied and the grapes will be at their peak, for the *fiesta* is scheduled for the night before she leaves."

"Then she's leaving fairly soon. I'm sorry to hear that; I had hoped we'd have time to get acquainted and perhaps go over to the little island together."

"I'll mention it to her." He shrugged and squared his sombrero to shade his face from the sun. "Maria tells me she spends most of her time chasing down to the shrimp boats to catch a glimpse of Juan, however. She seems more interested these days in that young man than in her sketching." With a chuckle, he led Gayle down a row of *cabernet sauvignon* vines, shaking his head good-naturedly as he walked.

By ten o'clock that morning the sun was high and hot rays poured heat down on the vineyard. "Your skin is too fair to stay outside any longer," Fernando told Gayle gravely. "It's time I took you to the main building."

Ramon had asked her to meet him in the blending room, saying he would be working there alone while Fernando was showing her around the vineyard. When Gayle found him, however, he was neither working nor alone, for Dianne Bennett, wearing hip-hugging, persimmon-colored slacks and a white halter, was strutting her lovely body all around the room taking pictures.

"You're just in time," she greeted Gayle. "Ramon tells me you'll be working here, so let me get a picture of you. Over there, by the wine bottles." She pointed a long tapered finger toward the blending table. "Take a glass in your hand and pretend to be tasting the wine or whatever it is one does here. I need to get a bit of action in some of these shots." She shrugged her bare shoulders, wrinkling her nose in a grimace of disgust. "So far this boss of yours has been totally uncooperative. He's really as unbending as a yardstick this morning," she added, silvery tones of teasing laughter bubbling through her vividly colored lips.

"Don't waste time chattering, Dianne," Ramon replied to her jibing. "You've thirty minutes more for your picture taking and that's all, if you want to get to Hermosillo in time for the plane back to New York this afternoon."

Gayle would swear that Dianne had flinched at the cool finality in his voice. But she lowered her head quickly over her camera and appeared to concentrate on the view finder, thus making it look as if she were unruffled by Ramon's caustic tone. Gayle sensed that the same underlying tension that had existed between Dianne and Ramon yesterday was still present today. Curiosity about their relationship sifted through her mind. She ran her hand underneath the back of her hair and rubbed the tense muscles of her neck. Why did it bother her so much? Was it because she felt attracted to Ramon herself? How ridiculous, she scoffed inwardly.

Quickly, she walked over and stood in front of the table of wines as Dianne had suggested. For another ten minutes, Dianne kept busy taking a rapid series of pictures. When she finished, she put her camera in its leather case, slung it over her shoulder and walked toward the door.

"So long," she tossed out her farewell. "I'll send along a dozen copies of *Renown* when the Albariza Wines issue comes out." She directed her statement to Ramon. "It's all here," she continued, patting her hand against the camera case. "Albariza Wines as they are and as they will forever remain—and you with them, my darling. *Viva* Mexico." Her voice held the brittle quality of forced bravado.

Ramon crossed to her, placing his hand on her arm to detain her. "If you or your father change your mind about doing this story," he paused, and looked intently into her face, "I'll understand, Dianne." He spoke to her in a quiet voice. "After all, I do know how unimportant my little corner of Mexico seems to you."

Her lips trembled, but she forced them into a thin smile. "You're news, darling, no matter where you are. And your wine conglomerate is bigger news yet. Daddy would never pass up such a story. We all know that, don't we?" Her voice was cold and her eyes shone like brown agates. "I never denied that your Mexican grape kingdom was a charming place to visit; I only said it would stifle me to live here." With these parting words, she walked from the room. Ramon made no effort to follow her. He watched her leave, then remained facing the doorway for another moment, his eyes expressionless.

Gayle kept her eyes on Ramon, wondering what his true reactions might be to Dianne's parting words. Was he in love with her? If not now, had he been at some time before this? Was she the real reason for his prejudices against American women? Had he wanted her to stay in Bahía Kino with him and had she refused because she found it stifling and dull? She recalled Ramon's remarks yesterday when he had told Dianne so contemptuously that he knew she would have a round trip ticket back to New York. There did seem to be some contest of wills going on between the two of them, that much was undeniable. She looked at Ramon, trying to read in his face the answer to how deeply he was affected by Dianne Bennett's leavetaking.

"Well now, Gayle," he returned her questioning stare, "I hardly think the aftermath of Dianne's act is quite that spellbinding. So why don't you stop gaping and get ready to go to work?" His manner was a curt dismissal of what had just taken place. He strode past her across the room.

"I—I didn't mean to stare—actually, I—"

"Put this on and be quiet," he interrupted, taking a white lab smock from a shelf and handing it to her.

She clamped her lips together, suppressing the irritation that welled up inside her at his brusque treatment, and followed his instructions. As soon as he had also donned a smock, he joined her at the blending table. The first day of her training at Albariza Wines had begun.

Over the next two weeks, she became well acquainted with the laboratory and the spotlessly clean blending table where thirty dark green glass bottles were lined in a single row. Each six-ounce bottle was stopped with a cork and contained a sample of wine which presently was stored in barrels, in cooperage, as it was called, within the Albariza winery. Some of the wines were very young, others had mellowed in oak barrels for as long as three years. One group of wines represented by the sample bottles had been fermented more quickly than the others, using temperature management to control the rate of fermentation.

Because Gayle was aware that Ramon was as highly skilled an enologist as Charlie Cartwright, and because Maria had told her of Ramon's desire to produce a wine from his grapes that was comparable to the Spanish sherry she had tasted, she took careful note of the casks of wine from which he was now blending his Mexican sherry. It was, in fact, when Ramon was talking about and working with these particular wines that she saw something to admire in him, something that she had not known existed before: an infinite patience.

"How long have you been working on this particular wine?" she asked him one Friday afternoon when they were working late in the lab to finish some tests.

He narrowed his eyes thoughtfully. "I don't calculate in days and weeks, and if you intend to be a winemaker, you need to remember one thing. Wine is a living thing whose development can't be hurried." He looked at her and smiled. "I imagine Charlie Cartwright has told you that, and most assuredly your father has."

"Yes, but never in quite those words. I like your way of saying it." She put her elbows on the table and leaned her chin on her hands watching him. "Tell me what you're seeking in this blend."

Ramon had been making notes in one of the steel-jacketed notebooks in which he kept data on the various blends. He put down his pen and sat down beside her. "You know, of course, that in the blending process the desired sweetness, color and alcoholic strength are attained. Now, there are several types of sherries ranging from the very light, pale dry sherry with a delicate flavor, called *fino*, to a full, dark-colored sweet wine, the *oloroso* sherry. In between these two lies the blend I'm seeking, the *amontillado*. It's somewhat fuller than the *fino*, with more firmness, due to age, and with slightly more color. It's a clear, light amber with a nutty flavor, and, like my grandfather's sherry, it will have a firmness due to age and be medium sweet."

"And the grapes this year, do you think they'll equal those grown in the *albariza* soil of Spain?" She stood up and reached for a bottle of wine on the blending table that had yet to be checked, and uncorked it.

"How did you know about the *albariza* soil?" he asked, eyeing her curiously.

107

Gayle was measuring a precise amount of wine with a cylindrical glass tube, taking it from the small bottle on the blending table and transferring it to a glass. She finished the operation before answering Ramon's question. "Maria told me. She mentioned going to Spain with you and your parents when you were a child."

Ramon came over to where she stood and took the glass from her hand, holding it up to the light and examining the wine critically. "The sherry district of Spain is fascinating. My father took me back twice after I was grown." He swirled the contents of the glass in his hand. "Good color," he muttered. "Here in Mexico, we employ the same techniques as in Spain." He continued swirling the wine in the glass as he spoke. "It's only that our grapes here have yet to produce wine of the refined delicacy of those grown in the hard, lime soil of Spain." He narrowed his eyes thoughtfully. "If you saw that Albariza vineyard, gleaming white in the sun and bone dry, you'd think it would be incapable of providing nourishment for any vegetation, least of all the grapevines." He smiled, reminiscing. "But I was there one year at the vintage and the vines were borne down with huge bunches of white grapes. You should have seen them." He smiled.

"I hope some day I can; I've never been to Spain."

He gave her a sidelong glance and she thought he was about to say something more about the Spanish vineyards. Instead, he bent his head over the glass he was holding and put his nose well over the rim, smelling the vapors. "Still a hint of off odor here," he commented. Passing the glass to Gayle, he reached for the notebook and began making further notations.

She wanted to discuss the *albariza* soil and the grapes used in the sherry wines further, but Ramon seemed to have dismissed the subject.

She was coming to realize that Ramon was a complex man with as many facets as a well-cut jewel. He was dedicated to making the finest possible wines here in Mexico, and to this end he demanded the total cooperation of all those who worked for him. Yet they all seemed to give it willingly. Indeed, the respect his employees felt for him at times bordered on reverence. She had seen how the young Mexicans who worked in the vineyards looked up to him.

Gayle could not deny his personal magnetism. In fact, she was more aware of him than she wanted to admit. At times, however, she found that working with him was like being on the light end of a seesaw. He often left her floundering high in the air with no apparent way to get her feet back on the ground. She suspected that he did this intentionally, to maintain his supremacy and emphasize his opinion that women had no place in the wine industry. His attitude toward her and his treatment of her varied, however, and she could not find an explanation for his ambivalence. Many days, as they worked together in the winery, he would actually volunteer intriguing information about the grapes. At these times, he took infinite pains to explain and illustrate so she would understand the reasons behind each method he employed. At the same time, he took an arrogant delight in dazzling her with a display of his own skills. As she learned from him and began to feel a sense of her own accomplishment, however, he would suddenly find fault with her and question her every opinion, usually disagreeing completely with her. If she said the wine was clear, then he found it to be vaguely cloudy. If she tasted a blend and found the flavor dry, he countered, saying it held a taint of sweetness.

At the *casa* he behaved toward her with the same conflicting attitude he had shown that first day on the plane, alternately personable and charming, then remote and preoccupied. Early mornings seemed to find him at his most congenial. She joined him for a swim before breakfast each morning, and Carmelita usually swam with them, too. The past two mornings, Carmelita had not appeared, however, so, on Saturday morning, when Carmelita ran along the sandy beach to catch up with them, Ramon greeted her with a teasing barb.

"You must have been staying out very late these last two nights since you couldn't get up early enough to swim with Gayle and me." He gave her a wry look. "I think I'll tell Juan you're two-timing him. While he's out all night on that shrimp boat of his, you're off with another fellow. Am I right?"

"You judge me far too quickly, Ramon." The girl's smoky brown eyes returned his gaze coolly.

"I was not judging you, *chiquita*." His manner was instantly friendly and open. "I'm sorry if I sounded as if I were."

"In that case, I'll tell you about it," she said, pursing her pretty mouth. "Juan couldn't take his boat out the past two nights. He had trouble with his engine and so I've been helping him work on it."

"I'll just bet she was some help, don't you Gayle?" He winked at her.

"Well, Juan got the engine repaired, and he

110

certainly had no objections to having me around."
Carmelita flung the words at Ramon as she pushed
several long strands of dark hair behind her ears.
Then, turning, she walked away from them, her
well-shaped body swaying with each step she took.
When she reached the deeper water she gracefully
let the waves carry her out.

Ramon followed her with his eyes until the brief
yellow bikini, and the girl in it, were hidden from
sight beneath the water. "The university is going to
be the best thing for that hot-blooded young lady,"
he said solemnly. "I can only hope it will settle her
down." He seemed to be talking more to himself
than to her, Gayle thought, so she didn't offer any
comment.

"Maria feels Carmelita sees too much of Juan."
He turned his attention to Gayle as he added this.
"It worries her that things might be getting serious
between them."

"And does it worry you, Ramon?" The question
seemed to form without her volition.

Ramon shot her a curious look. For several sec-
onds he said nothing. Then, still looking at her
intently, he said tersely, "I think we had better have
a swim or we'll be late for breakfast." Without
waiting for her, he strode across the sandy beach
toward the water.

She wondered why she had blurted out such a
question. She gazed after him, still feeling the sting
of his rebuff, knowing she had spoiled the usual
pleasantness of their morning swim together.

Later that morning, at the winery, she was relieved to find she would be alone in the blending
room for an hour or two. Ramon had joined Fer-

nando in the vineyards to select the sample of grapes that would be crushed and checked for sugar levels. Since Ramon's disposition hadn't improved following their swim, it would seem a little time and distance were needed to clear the air between them, and she hoped that, by the time he finished with the grapes and came to the lab, he would have forgotten the incident on the beach.

Taking the sample bottle of *Cabernet Sauvignon* and placing it on the table in front of her, she opened the notebook to read her final notations from the day before. She felt confident of her ability to evaluate this particular red wine, for she had had previous experience with it in her father's winery and she understood its flavor, richness and aroma as well as its aging ability. The *Cabernet Sauvignon* developed at Golden Valley was of exceptional quality, and Charlie had stressed its fine points with her many times. Today, she needed samples of some of the Mexican vintages which had been aging five years or more. Rather than wait for Ramon, she decided to go ask the cellar foreman for these herself. This early in the day she would be sure to find Pablo, the young assistant foreman in the cooperage area. Since he had come from one of the Texas border cities, he was one of the few Mexicans at Albariza Wines who spoke fluent English and with whom she could converse easily.

Knowing Ramon would spend most of the morning in the vineyards with Fernando, she felt no compulsion to return immediately to the blending room. So, after Pablo had collected the bottles of the red wine she had asked for, she continued to follow him as he made his rounds throughout the cellar and

AMBER WINE

questioned him about the vintages of the different wines.

"It certainly is cold in here," Gayle said, hugging herself and rubbing her bare arms briskly to warm them.

"It's always kept at fifty-eight degrees in this room," the Mexican explained. "The *señor* is very strict about that. We have to keep it uniform because we have champagne fermenting." Pablo quickly unzipped the tan cotton poplin jacket he was wearing over his work shirt. "Wear this, *señorita*. I'm so used to it, I don't mind the cold much." He held the jacket out so she could slip her arms into the sleeves. "It's too large for you; you're a small lady." He grinned at her, and his teeth were startlingly white in contrast to the tawny brown of his skin.

"It's fine," she said gratefully, wrapping the jacket snugly around her. "Thank you."

They continued walking and Pablo pointed out some of the wines that were aging in the traditional barrels of French oak. Gayle was enjoying having someone other than Ramon explain to her about the extensive storage and she forgot completely about the time. She was surprised to discover, when she finally did return to the blending room, that she had been gone more than an hour and a half. She was even more chagrined to find Ramon waiting for her, his expression one of obvious displeasure.

"Where have you been, Gayle?" The irritation in his voice matched his look. "I've been waiting half an hour for you."

"I—I'm sorry. I picked up some wine from the cellar."

"So I see. And did it take you all morning to get

113

three samples of wine?" His smooth dark eyes regarded her with disdain.

"Well . . ." she hesitated. He was certainly out of sorts, and she didn't want to annoy him further. "Pablo showed me some of the older vintages and then he took me with him while he checked the fermentation of the champagne," she explained with an apologetic smile. "I guess I stayed longer than I intended."

"Obviously," he snapped, as he took the three bottles from her and set them in place on the blending table.

"I got so interested in what Pablo was showing me and I—"

"Pablo, is it?" Ramon interrupted her rudely.

"Yes, he's the assistant cellar foreman."

"I know what his job is, Gayle. What I didn't know was that you were on such familiar terms with one of my employees," he retorted flatly, and his brows came together, black and furious.

The implied slur in his words made her flush with anger. Pressing her lips together, she suppressed a caustic reply. There was nothing to gain by letting Ramon know how upset he was making her. "I regret any delay I may have caused by not being here when you came up from the vineyards." She shifted nervously under his gaze. "Can't we just go to work now?"

He moved his shoulders in an offhand gesture, his eyes flicking over her with mocking insolence. "We can when you put on your lab coat. A man's jacket is hardly suitable attire for the work we need to do."

His statement made her suddenly aware that she was still wearing Pablo's jacket. "I—I forgot to give it back to Pablo," she stammered inanely as she awkwardly pulled her arms from the over long sleeves.

Ramon made no effort to assist her. "Surely you could have found something more attractive to wear?"

"You know how cold it is in the champagne cellar—only fifty-eight degrees. I was shivering, so Pablo offered to let me wear this. I thought it was very thoughtful of him." The words tumbled out of her mouth as she continued to struggle out of the jacket.

"I'm sure you were cold and I'm equally certain you would have preferred it if Pablo had found other ways to warm you rather than with his ill-fitting jacket." His dark features mirrored his contempt.

She stripped off the jacket in a sudden rush of fury. "That's such a ridiculous remark, I refuse to even comment on it." Turning her back on him, she started over to pick up her lab coat.

"Then allow me to comment on it further. I told you once before that I won't allow a woman to be a disruptive influence in my winery and I meant it." Grabbing hold of her shoulders, he turned her back to face him. "You do understand the point I'm making, don't you? You are not to disturb any of the men at Albariza Wines." The powerful line of his jaw was unyielding and his face was disturbingly close to hers.

Gayle found herself looking up at him quite against her will; he seemed to hold her with the hypnotic stare of his dark eyes as well as with the firm pressure of his hands. He pulled her against him and for a moment she could not speak; the passion in his eyes staggered her and a tremor of strong emotion raced through her body. She clenched her fists

115

tight against the sides of her body, fighting to check
the stirring excitement that his nearness was making
her feel. A sudden rush of pure fury came to her
rescue, loading her mind with the ammunition she
needed to get back at him in kind. Parting her lips
slightly, she let her breath out in a sensuous sigh.

"From your words and actions, I believe the only
man at Albariza Wines who finds me disturbing is
you." She paused to add emphasis to her statement.
"You will let me know if I bother *you* in *any way*,
won't you?" Saying the words softly, she tilted her
face a fraction as her lips were almost touching his.

A shadow of surprise crossed his face and she felt
the rigid tightening of his muscles. The tensing of a
muscle at the side of his mouth also revealed his
tension. In a second, however, a knowing smile
moved slowly across his lips and he began to gently
knead the soft flesh of her shoulders with his warm
hands. "I'll do more than just let you know, *señorita*
—much more." He spoke the words against her lips
and his mouth was so close to hers that she could
almost believe he had kissed her fleetingly.

He released her, taking his hands from her shoulders with a seeming reluctance at the same time as
he moved his face away from hers with a tantalizing
slowness that unnerved her. "We seem to have
arrived at an impasse. At least for the time being,"
he said, pushing his hands into the pockets of his lab
coat. Walking past her, he picked up her lab coat and
held it out to her.

She did not speak. Indeed, at this moment, she
did not trust herself to say anything at all. Strange
new emotions that she didn't understand stirred
wildly inside her. Taking the white coat from him,

she put it on. Her fingers shook as she struggled to push the flat plastic buttons through the buttonholes, which suddenly seemed too small. Somehow, she managed to accomplish the task and, carefully keeping her eyes averted from Ramon's, she approached the blending table and started to work.

Chapter Seven

Ramon didn't refer to their argument and the day
progressed in a state of unspoken truce. At breakfast
the following morning, he seemed so congenial that
Gayle could almost believe he had forgotten the
incident, or else thought it too trivial to be mentioned again. He was in such good humor that he
even directed some of his considerable charm to
Maria as she busily served their bacon and eggs.

"What kind of wine should I take to complement
the lunch you're packing? It must do justice to your
good food."

Maria turned a pleased face to him. "A chablis
would suit, or a rosé, but be sure to chill it," she
cautioned. "I have cheese tacos for you and, of
course, *biscochitos*." Her bright eyes tilted in a
smile. "That's a Mexican cookie with anise seeds
that I think you'll particularly enjoy," she said,
turning to Gayle as she described it.

Gayle felt a shiver of surprised delight racing through her. "What are you talking about? A picnic?"

"It was Maria's suggestion. Does the idea appeal to you?"

"Of course it does. It sounds wonderful." She looked up from her breakfast and smiled at Maria. It was so unexpected, and even if the picnic hadn't actually been Ramon's idea, still, the prospect of doing something special with him on this Sunday pleased her.

"I told Señor Ramon it was time he showed you something of our country," the Mexican woman said firmly. She used the same tone she used with Fernando and Gayle felt inwardly amused. Maria managed to have her way about everything here at Casa del Mar, there was no doubt about that. She managed the good-natured Fernando with wifely finesse, and she manipulated Ramon without his even knowing it, and that was quite an accomplishment for any woman. Gayle smiled at the thought.

"Would you like to see the Seri Indian village at Punta Chueca? We could do that and then have lunch on the nearby shell beach. How does that sound to you?" Ramon's question brought her attention back to the present.

"Could we?"

"We could." He smiled, reaching for another piece of toast. "And if the Seris have some carvings ready to sell, I'll buy you a *palofierro figuro*."

"What is a *palofierro figuro*?" She tried to give the words the same rolling intonation he had used.

"It's a carving made from ironwood."

"Ironwood? I never heard of it before." She took a sip of her coffee and went on. "What exactly is it?"

119

"It's an extremely hard wood. Hard as iron." He eyed her with an amused grin. "I can see I have a lot to show you," he chuckled. "This wood is so hard, in fact, that the Seri men cut the rough shapes for their carvings with an ax or a machete, and it's called ironwood because of its dark, rusted-iron color and its heavy weight."

Gayle put her fork down on her plate, too interested in what Ramon was telling her to eat. "What sort of things do they carve? Indian men and women?"

Ramon shook his head. "Never human figures, and for some strange reason, never toys or dolls. They always carve the things they're highly familiar with, sharks, sailfish, turtles, pelicans, and even the gulls and roadrunners."

Her eyes widened and she leaned across the table toward him. "I would love to have a pelican. Did you know it was the first bird I saw that afternoon when Fernando was driving me here from the vineyards? There were several of them, flying in a sort of squadron formation, and then one by one they peeled off like dive bombers to zoom down into the water. They were after fish to eat, Fernando told me." Her blue eyes sparkled as if picturing the sight again. "I know later on, whenever I think of being here at Bahía Kino, it will be the pelican I'll remember first."

Ramon pushed his chair back from the table and tossed his napkin down beside his plate. "*Qué lástima!* What a pity, eh, Maria?" He shook his head, feigning remorse. "Maria, our American *señorita* here finds a pelican more memorable than Casa del Mar or my beautiful vineyards."

"I didn't mean that. You know that wasn't what I

meant at all!" she protested, feeling flustered by his teasing.

His dark eyes reflected his laughter. He was obviously amused by her reaction. "Well, since it means that much to you, you shall have it. I promise I will get a Seri carving of a pelican this very day and place it in those pretty little hands of yours." He stood behind her chair, with his hands resting lightly on her shoulders. "I need to warn you, however, it's twenty miles to the Seri village over a road that's very little more than a path across the desert. It will take us over an hour to drive it." He touched the bare skin at the back of her neck as he spoke and let his fingers brush through the soft ends of her hair.

His touch sent a flutter along her pulses. She trembled. It frightened her that she reacted so to Ramon's slightest touch.

With his hand still fingering her hair, he said, "Better bring along a hat. Your light hair and skin need to be shaded from the hot sun."

"I'm glad you reminded me," she smiled up at him. "I've got a wide-brimmed straw one I'll bring with me."

He pulled her chair back from the table. "Get it, then, and meet me at the car in fifteen minutes." His manner had become suddenly brusque.

What had happened? What had she done wrong? It was as if Ramon had at that instant remembered something to make him angry. Without a further word to Maria or to her, he turned and walked purposefully from the kitchen. Ramon's lightning quick changes mystified her. Maybe it had been the mention of blond hair and fair skin. Had that made him think of his mother? And had he taken out his resentment of her on Gayle? Or had it been something altogether different? Did he all of a sudden resent the thought of spending the day with her? She rubbed her hand across the back of her neck, still absurdly conscious of how gentle and warm Ramon's hand had felt. Somehow, she must restore his earlier good humor or the day would be impossible. Letting a Mona Lisa smile curve the corners of her mouth, she vowed to find a way to do exactly that.

The road to Punta Chueca was, if anything, worse than Ramon had indicated. The small, maroon sports car jolted over every rut and rock, making Gayle feel as if she were a soft ball being bounced off a hard paddle. As they drew near the village she caught sight of some of the dark-skinned Seri women wearing long, colorful cotton skirts with overblouses of vivid shades.

"Nobody seems to wear shoes," she remarked to Ramon.

"Shoes are expensive and the sandy soil is warm." He shrugged.

Ramon stopped the car near some huts where a group of the Seri men were shaping wood with machete knives and a rasp. Nearby, a dozen or more women were either painstakingly sanding the wood carvings or polishing them with repeated applications of wax.

No sooner had Ramon turned off the engine than four of the women approached, thrusting carvings of various shapes and sizes through the car window.

"What on earth are they saying?" Gayle asked, hearing the high-pitched dialect of the Seri women.

"They have their own characteristic speech, but I can usually make them understand me. You just smile and act friendly and I'll deal with them."

She nodded, and edged closer to him. Ramon leaned out the car window, gesturing toward the oldest woman of the group, for she appeared to be the matriarch. The brown-faced Seri extended her hand toward him and Gayle could see that she held a carving of a long, sharp-finned shark. The gleaming waxed sheen of the dark wood was beautiful to behold.

"No—no shark—no *tiburón*." He shook his head at her. "Other *palofierro figuros—sí?* he asked, pointing to the woven straw basket that one of the other Indian women had placed on the ground by the old woman's bare feet. "Have you a pelican in your basket?"

The old Seri frowned, her jet black eyes questioning and her forehead a map of wrinkles.

"Pelican—*figuro de alcatraz.*" Ramon said the Spanish words slowly.

Her eyes were round and shiny as two black jet beads. Bending over, she thrust her wrinkled hand among the objects in the basket. Each carving appeared to be individually wrapped in a soft rag. For a few moments, the elderly woman poked through them, feeling the different objects to determine their shape beneath the cloth. Eventually, she pulled one out and removed the covering. When she held it up, Gayle could see that it was a beautifully proportioned pelican, about eight inches in height. Drawing in her breath, she let it out again in a sigh of delight. "It's beautiful—it's perfect, Ramon," she whispered.

"*El figuro—cuanto es?*" Pulling his billfold from his hip pocket, he removed several bills to illustrate his intention to buy.

Instantly, a volley of words issued from the woman's thin lips. Surprisingly, the shrill Indian dialect disappeared and the woman now found a vast number of understandable Spanish words to speak to Ramon in order to obtain a handsome price for the ironwood carving. Gayle found the situation highly amusing, for the woman bargained shrewdly; she was obviously a skilled huckster. When the price was agreed upon, the Seri woman carefully rubbed the carving with the cloth in which it had been wrapped and, when its waxed surface was free of fingerprints she passed it through the car window to Gayle, a smile mellowing her aged face.

"It's beautiful." Gayle's voice rang with pleasure on beholding the carving at close range. Bending her head, she examined the intricate grain of the dark brown wood. "Ramon, thank you. I love it," she murmured, as the old woman shuffled away from the car. Gayle rubbed her fingers over the polished surface, liking the satiny feel of the wood.

Glancing up, she discovered Ramon watching her with a bemused expression. "Is your pelican like the one you saw over the water that first afternoon?" The deep timbre of his voice sounded soothing to her ears after the shrill chatter of the Seri woman.

"I believe it could be the very one," she laughed easily, feeling comfortable with him now. "When I have to leave Mexico, I'll have my pelican to remind me of your paradise on the Sea of Cortez."

Ramon's ebony eyes searched her face and she could feel her cheeks flush under his scrutiny. He must think her childish to carry on so over a simple carving. She lowered her head and again traced the markings in the wood grain.

"Are you telling me there are aspects about Bahía Kino you will wish to remember?" He leaned toward her, touching his fingers underneath her chin and tilting her face up to his.

"Of course there are. Many things." She said the words as calmly as she could manage under the circumstances, although the touch of his fingers was affecting her noticeably. She kept her eyes averted from his. "I shall wish to remember all the beautiful things here, as well as the people, all those who have been friendly and considerate to me," she sputtered. What little composure she had now dissolved, for his face was disconcertingly close to hers.

"And who are they?" Ramon's eyes glittered with amusement as he deliberately tilted her head a little higher.

"Maria, Fernando, Carmelita," she rattled off their names quickly, then deliberately hesitated, lifting her eyes to meet his laughing gaze. He was teasing her, so she would show him two could play that game.

"Is that your way of telling me again that I've been a poor host, even after I managed to acquire the carving you wanted?"

She caught a glimpse of something serious in the depth of his eyes. Maybe it was only her imagination, but somehow she felt he was not teasing her now. Did it actually matter to him that she felt he had shown her little consideration while she had been at Casa del Mar?

"Ramon, you've arranged an interesting, even exciting, day for me today, and you were thoughtful and considerate to get the pelican for me." Her words were uneven and she found it difficult to speak because of the way he was looking at her. "I had forgotten that I criticized you before," she added quickly.

125

"Had you forgotten? I don't really think you had, Gayle. I do intend, though, to change my image in your eyes." A smile slowly curved his mouth.

She drew back slightly, needing to find refuge in the corner recess of the seat. She even tried to pull her head away, but his fingers were too firm on her chin. Involuntarily, she closed her eyes, trembling because a feeling she could not identify, or perhaps was afraid to, was spreading over her. She wanted Ramon to touch her, hold her. It was frightening to be so aware of the power he had to attract her.

"Your lovely mouth is trembling, *señorita.* I could make it stop." He took his hand from her chin and laid a finger against her lips. "But, unfortunately, this is not exactly the time or the place." He took his hand from her face with obvious reluctance. "Let's get out of here." Sliding back behind the wheel, he turned the key in the ignition and they turned around, heading away from the Indian village.

Gayle sat silent, huddled in the corner of the seat, cradling the pelican in her hands. She tried to make her mind a blank, for that was the only thing that might help her still the clamor of her pounding heart. What was happening to her? Why did Ramon's slightest touch affect her so?

After only a few miles, Ramon swung the car onto an even narrower road and she realized this must be the shell beach he had mentioned this morning. "We'll have to park up here and walk down to the water." He switched off the motor. "The sand can be treacherous here and it's easy to get stuck if you drive too close to the water."

"You sound as if you knew that from experience," she said, getting quickly out of the car.

"As a matter of fact, I do. I got stuck here on this

beach last October and had to stay overnight until Fernando figured out what must have happened and came to tow me out with one of the trucks from the vineyard." He handed her the picnic basket while he took the cooler and some fishing tackle from the trunk of the car. "It wouldn't have been so bad, except I was out here all alone. Now today, for example, with you here to keep me company, I wouldn't mind a bit." His eyes swept over her with a warm, appraising look.

Without commenting, she started down the sandy incline to the water's edge. The aura of excitement that hung between them was dangerous, unsettling, and she felt caught off guard. Ramon had maintained a businesslike rapport with her these past few weeks, as they worked together in the lab at the winery. Today, though, it was becoming apparent, he was putting their relationship on a different basis. Merely thinking about it made her pulse quicken.

As they drew near the water, Ramon walked beside her, and their shoulders brushed against each other's as they moved slowly along the wide expanse of beach. It was level and smooth now, for the tide had swept it clean. Just ahead, two huge rocks formed two sides of a triangular shelter. "We'll eat here and we can use these boulders as a backrest." Ramon set the cooler down on the sand and took the basket from Gayle. She sat down Indian fashion, tucking her legs under her. The sand felt warm, but not uncomfortably so, and her jeans protected her legs from the sharp bits of seashells which had been crushed into the sand.

Ramon leaned back against one of the rocks, stretching his long legs out in front of him. Comfortably settled, Gayle took two of the tacos from the basket beside her, handing one to Ramon. Biting into the crisp *tortilla*, she discovered that the smooth taste of the cheese filling was sparked with a hot pepper sauce. It was delicious. She ate with relish, for not only was she hungry, but Maria's Mexican food was a spicy treat. Ramon, too, seemed to be relishing the tacos, so they ate in silence, watching the wind make circles on the water. It struck Gayle that this was the first time she and Ramon had been together in such a casual, relaxed atmosphere. She was beginning to feel at ease with him, and she liked that, for she realized that he had become very important in her life.

As if he sensed what she was thinking, he reached for another taco and said, "You like the shell beach, don't you?" The way he said it, she felt it was as much a statement as a question.

"I think it has me mesmerized. It's so tranquil and remote."

"Do you mean you find it lonely?" He leaned his shoulders back against the rock again.

"No, not lonely." She shook her head, wondering why he had asked her that question.

"Maria is quite fond of you."

Jarred by Ramon's abrupt change of topic, she quickly swallowed the last bite of the crisp tortilla, which seemed to have stuck in her throat. "I—I'm glad. I like her, too."

"Your amber beauty fulfills one of her fantasies."

"What do you mean?" She blinked her eyes in surprise at his strange words.

Ramon leaned forward, and she thought he was reaching for something more to eat. Instead, he cupped her face gently in his hands. Her breath caught and held, as if she were afraid to shatter this moment that hung between them, fragile as a silken cobweb.

"I mean it makes Maria happy to have a lovely blond in the blue room at Casa del Mar once again." His eyes narrowed slightly.

"She was devoted to your mother . . . I sensed that." She let her breath out in a sigh.

"We were all devoted to her. My father worshipped her. But it was never enough." His fingers pressed her cheeks more firmly. She beheld in him a capacity for emotion she had not seen before. It was there in his eyes, and in the taut muscles of his body, and she could feel it in the hands holding her face. "My mother *resided* at Casa del Mar, she never truly lived there." Harshness hardened his voice. "You Americans, you don't like Mexico and you refuse to adapt to our ways!" How bitter he sounded, and his strong hands formed a painful vise, crushing her face.

"Ramon," she winced, "you're hurting me!" Jerking away, she sprang to her feet. "Why must you always generalize about Americans? We're not all alike and we don't all feel or act the same." Her chin squared obstinately. "I, for one, like what I've seen of Mexico. Certainly the vineyards are impressive, and Casa Del Mar is so beautiful I can't believe *any* woman wouldn't want to live there." Anger made her voice soar. "Did you ever stop to think that the fault could be yours? You refuse to accept Americans, Ramon. At least, American women. If your father was like you, then maybe he never gave your mother a chance to belong and be a part of your life here." She spun away from him and started off along the beach. "I'm going to collect some shells," she hollered back over her shoulder, then trudged away

129

from him, kicking angrily at the sand with the toes of her tennis shoes as she went. She didn't want to hear anything more he might feel inclined to say.

She kept her eyes down, staring absently at the marks her feet made in the wet sand. Angry tears stung her eyes. For a short time it had seemed that this day held such happy promise. Why had Ramon spoiled it for her, spoiled it, in fact, for both of them?

Walking more slowly, she bent over to retrieve a tiny, perfect conch shell of a delicate pink color. In an attempt to push aside the depression that had settled on her, she concentrated on scanning the beach for shells. In a short time she had found a deeply ridged shell with a pearlized interior, two smaller ones in a golden brown tortoiselike color and a double coral shell still hinged together so that it opened and closed like a tiny box. Taking off her straw hat, she turned it upside down so she could use it as a basket to carry her collection. Finding another shell of an intriguing deep purple, she squatted down to dip it in the water and rinse the sand and dried seaweed from it. When it was clean, she discovered that the inner part was a lovely shade of lavender, making it look as if it were lined with a petal from a light purple iris.

The sound of the gulls swooping down, dipping into the sea in search of food, made her look out over the blue-green water. She shaded her eyes with one hand and peered back down the beach. She hadn't realized she had come so far. Ramon appeared like a small, thin figure, standing upright at the water's edge. She guessed he was fishing, but it was difficult to tell from this distance.

Still staring off down the beach, she became aware of the shuffling sound of footsteps in the sand behind her. Startled, she whirled around to see a giant of a man moving rapidly toward her. Her mouth flew open to cry out, but she was totally unable to utter a sound. She stood there, paralyzed with panic, as the Seri man towered over her, his long, straight black hair framing his coarse features like a cowl. He muttered several strange sounding words and took another step toward her. It was then that she caught sight of the long knife sticking out of the pocket of his dirt stained khaki trousers.

Wild terror spiraled through her. What did he want? Was he going to harm her? The Indian was staring into her face, his expression grimly stolid. Then the savage-looking man put out his hand, almost as if he were asking for something. Then he raised his hand and she thought he intended to strike her. She screamed. She struggled to lift her feet but it seemed as if ten pound weights were tied to each leg. Panic soared inside her and she managed to run, but everything seemed to be happening in an agony of slow motion. The harder she struggled, the slower she seemed to move.

"Ramon!" She screamed his name, her voice filled with hysteria. Uncontrollable tears streamed down her face. The wind blew her pale hair across her face and several strands clung to her wet cheeks. She stumbled along, barely able to keep from falling. She ran faster now, at last conscious that Ramon was racing down the beach toward her. Suddenly, she knew she had escaped as she felt the blessed strength of Ramon's arms crushing her body to his and she collapsed against the warm safety of his chest.

"Gayle! What happened! Are you all right?" His lips were against her temple as he spoke. "Who was that man on the beach with you?"

"He—he had a knife. One of those huge, horrible knives. I thought he was going to kill me." Another spasm of sobs racked her body.

"It's all right. You're safe. You're with me now." He smoothed her hair back from her tear-covered face. "He probably was just a Seri from the village," Ramon said, tightening his arms around her. "They carry those knives for their carvings. You even saw them cutting the ironwood with them." He talked to her slowly, his words quiet. "He probably wanted to ask you for food or drinking water. They often beg from the fishermen. Why, I imagine you frightened him, with all your screaming, as much as he scared you." Ramon caressed her back to comfort and soothe her. "He's gone now, and no one is going to hurt you, *querida mia.*"

She didn't understand the Spanish words, but she instinctively felt that the soft inflection of his voice wasn't mocking, and certainly he wasn't calling her *"señorita"* in that belittling way he had so often used before.

"Querida," he said again. She felt the warmth of his breath against her hair, and with the fright over the Seri pushed from her thoughts, she now became acutely conscious of the hands moving over her back and shoulders.

She had stopped crying. She took a deep breath, inhaling Ramon's male scent, discovering it was a pleasing combination of soap and shaving lotion. He stroked her shoulders, then moved his hands down her arms. His fingers were warm and familiar on her suntanned skin. His lips brushed against her temple, sending a pleasing shiver along the top of her cheek bone, like the touch of a downy feather. She could feel her pulse quicken beneath his lips. "You're better now, Gayle." He held her slightly away from him, just far enough to look into her upturned face.

She felt on fire now with new sensations, for his lips were so close to hers that there was no denying the emotions that raged between them. Willingly, she melted closer to him, letting the soft curves of her body mold themselves to the muscled strength of his. She wanted him to kiss her more than she had ever wanted anything before, and she knew that he wanted it too, for desire flamed in his black eyes. His mouth came down, possessing hers. Lifting her hands to circle his neck, she clung to him, her lips parted under the persuasive pressure of his mouth. Feeling the hard pounding of his heart against her breast, she welcomed the crushing strength of his arms enfolding her, protecting her. Here in Ramon's embrace, she knew there was nothing that could harm her. The kiss deepened and she moaned softly against his lips. She was oblivious to place and time and everything in the world except his mouth exploring the softness of hers.

Without being aware of how it happened, she felt herself sinking down as Ramon pulled her with him. Now the warm, smooth sand was beneath her back. Unleashed passion flamed between them, and Ramon's hands moved over her with an increasing intimacy, bringing all her senses vibrantly alive.

"I want you, Gayle. You're beautiful and soft." He rasped out the words as his lips found the deep, white hollow between her breasts.

She felt on fire with emotions she had never even known existed, and she held his head pressed warmly to her.

"My word, you're an exciting, amber witch."

She trembled violently as his words penetrated her euphoric state. He had called her an amber witch before, and it had been with furious censure in his voice. Though he hadn't used it viciously this time, hearing the words somehow frightened and upset her.

Maybe it was that, or maybe it was that her mind suddenly began to combat her own uncontrolled physical response to Ramon's lovemaking, but she forced herself to move her hands from his head and placed her palms flat against his shoulders. She tried to push him away with what strength she could manage.

"Ramon," she whispered unevenly, "please—let me go now." She tried to slide away from him but she only seemed to burrow deeper in the sand. His arms tightened in protest at her attempted withdrawal. "Please—I—I can't—" Her voice broke off in a breathless cry.

His brows came together, his eyes flashing darkly, desire for her mirrored in their black depths. Slowly, he released her and, propping himself on one elbow, scrutinized her face. He stared at her for a long moment before he spoke. "I'm curious, Gayle." His voice was razor sharp. "The Seri didn't really frighten you all that much, did he?

She stared at him, totally baffled by his words.

"Wasn't that terrified flight of yours only an excuse to throw your lovely body against mine so you could prove you had the feminine powers to inflame a man's passion?" His eyes were hard and cold.

"I—I don't know what you mean," she gasped. She was not only astonished by what he was saying but frightened by his sneering sarcasm.

"Oh, I think a provocative American girl like you knows exactly what I mean. All that quaking fear of yours was an act to enable you to prove to yourself that even though you'd been rejected by your California lawyer, you still had the charms to attract another man. I just happened to be a convenient target—as did Pablo, the other day."

Complete disbelief stopped her breathing. It was inconceivable. Ramon could not know anything about Ken. "How—how did you . . . ?" She sucked in her breath, but frustration and anger made it impossible for her to force the words through her lips.

As if he knew exactly what she was thinking, he said, "Your father told me you needed to get over a disappointing love affair. That's how, Gayle."

"He had no business telling you anything about my personal life!" She could feel her face flushing with painful embarrassment. She brushed angry tears from her eyes. How could her father have been so callous and unthinking as to tell Ramon she had been jilted? She cringed with shame. "I'm appalled," she said running her tongue across her lips. "I can't understand why my own father would do such a thing to me. Why he would tell a stranger that." She blinked her eyes to fight back further tears.

"I asked him, that's why," Ramon said with unconcerned matter-of-factness.

She glared at him. "Why were you so interested in my lovers, or lack of them?" Her voice was as brittle as cracking ice.

"I told you before, there's no place in the wine industry for flighty women, and I wanted to make sure you'd not disrupt work by flying back to California to visit some man every time you got tired of the hard work here."

She tried to sit up, but when she did, he leaned over her so she couldn't get up without coming into close contact with him again. "I haven't disrupted any of the work at Albariza Wines!" She hurled her words up at him. "If you were man enough to admit it, you'd have to say I've worked hard and already learned a good deal about blending your wines."

"And if I admit that," his lips curved in a mocking smile, "then what?"

"Then you'll stop calling me a 'frivolous American female' or an 'amber witch.' I don't deserve either one of those, or any other nasty label, either."

He deliberately lowered his face closer to hers. "When I discover exactly what goes on in that golden head of yours," he touched the light hair that framed her face, pushing it away from her cheeks, "and what you feel here in your heart," he brushed his hand across her breast, "then I'll know exactly what name to give you." The anger was not as evident in his voice now as it had been, yet there was something enigmatic about what he said. She didn't understand him, and certainly she never seemed able to fathom that strange ambivalence he continued to feel for her.

He stood up then, and, taking both her hands in his, he pulled her to her feet. "Your skin looks as if it may already have gotten too much sun. I'm going to take you home." They stood facing each other, and he looked at her, a strange half smile curving his mouth. He didn't let go of her hands, and for some odd reason, this slight contact between them sent a radiant heat flowing through her veins again.

"Ramon," she said softly, "I really was frightened by the Indian. Escaping from him and that horrible knife was the only thought in my mind."

His eyes searched hers with cool conjecture. After a long moment, he dropped her hands and, turning away, walked over to the rock shelter and began to gather up the picnic basket. She followed him in silence.

Just then a large pelican swooped down and landed at the water's edge, only a few feet from the rocks. The bird stood there, preening its feathers. Surprisingly enough, their movements as they picked up the picnic basket and the fishing tackle didn't frighten the pelican. Rather, he appeared unafraid of them, and contented to share the beach with them. Gayle watched the graceful bird with his deep pouch of a beak, knowing that, to her, he was a symbol of the enchantment of Mexico. She had felt his power that first day, driving to Casa del Mar. She felt it even more strongly now.

Ramon handed her the basket and, without commenting, the two of them headed for the car. As they climbed the sandy hill to get from the beach to the road, Gayle stole a glance at Ramon's profile. How unpredictable his actions were. She wondered if she would ever understand his varied moods. She wondered, too, if he would ever take her in his arms again, as he had there on the beach. Had he desired her because she was herself, or had she been only a substitute for the absent Dianne? Was Ramon in love with Dianne Bennett? Surely something was going on between them. She gasped as a sharp stab of jealousy hit her.

"Am I walking too fast for you?" Ramon stopped and waited for her to resume breathing easily.

Clearing her throat, she swallowed the knot of pain that had choked her when she thought of the prior claim Dianne appeared to have on Ramon's affections. "I—I guess I got a little winded," she stammered. "I'm all right now."

As they walked on, he slowed his steps, and she knew he was trying to make the climb easier for her. She could feel her heart pounding hard in her breast, but she knew it was from more than the effort of walking up the sandy hillside. She could no longer question her own emotions, for they were too strong to allow any room for doubt. She was in love with Ramon, ardently and profoundly in love, though heaven alone knew why. He was always turning on her, he seemed not to care for her at all, but even so, it was exciting and magical and more than a little frightening.

With a sidelong glance, she took in the strong, angular planes of his face. It now seemed to her that she might have been falling in love with him from that first day on the plane. Certainly she had experienced his compelling magnetism when he had warned her, outside the customs office, that he wouldn't allow a woman to disrupt his life and the work of his winery. Instead it was *her* life that had been disrupted, and by *him*. He had entered her life and touched her body and her mind and her emotions, arousing feelings in her she had never known before. She trembled, for the power of her feelings both surprised and frightened her.

138

Soaring, exciting sensations filled her with love and desire for Ramon, but it wasn't enough, she wanted more. She wanted, needed, the security of *his* love in return. Quickening her steps, she moved ahead of him so she could no longer see his profile. What would she do if Ramon should never love her? Her eyes burned with unshed tears.

Chapter Eight

Once the harvesting of the grapes began, there was a crescendo of excitement throughout the vineyards. This was the best of times, for the grapes had matured exactly on the schedule Fernando had predicted. This meant that the fiesta could be held the night before Carmelita was to leave for the university, and this fact seemed to be of the utmost importance to the entire household at Casa del Mar.

"Carmelita has never missed a wine festival in her entire life," Fernando told Gayle, a broad grin on his round face. "And we could not let her miss it this year. Why, she was only seven months old that very first time. I'll never forget it." Taking off his sombrero, he wiped the sweat from his face. "Maria gave me such a tongue-lashing because I dipped my hand in the new wine and let the baby suck my fingers. Maria was so sure it would give Carmelita the colic." He laughed and put his hat back on. "Do you know, Carmelita sucked my fingers, cooed softly and promptly went to sleep and slept through the entire evening." He laughed again. "As a matter of fact, as the wine flowed freely and the laughter and singing reached a noisy peak, my little one, my *chiquita,* she slept contentedly through it all." Shrugging as he recalled the event to Gayle, he chuckled. "A papa knows best, right? And a taste of good Albariza wine, that's a blessing as well as a treat." He smiled at her, and as he left her to return to his work, she heard his tuneful whistling.

Gayle dressed carefully for the fiesta. It was the first opportunity she'd had since coming to Mexico to dress up and be a part of a social occasion. Besides, with all the feverish excitement and the gala preparations that had been going on at the vineyard, she was in an expectant, party mood. She was glad that she had packed something feminine and pretty. She would like to merit an admiring glance. Maybe even Ramon, who had been cold and distant with her lately, would notice her anew in her finery. Pulling curlers from her freshly washed hair, she brushed it to let the pale golden curls frame her face and the shining length touch her shoulders. Taking another look at herself, she added a final touch of mascara to her lashes and a dash of shadow to her eyelids to further accent the blue of her eyes. Pleased with the effect, she uncapped a new bottle of her favorite perfume. It was one Ken had given her several months ago, for her birthday. She remembered it had been a gift from him, but for some reason the fact now seemed unimportant, actually inconsequential. She applied the lovely floral fragrance to her temples, along her throat, and across the top of her bare shoulders. She felt free of the past tonight, and her love for Ramon, hopeless as it seemed to be, had at least done that for her. She wouldn't want to return to Ken now under any circumstances. She parted her lips in a wistful sigh, thinking that if she wanted to return to any place, it would be to the shell beach with Ramon. Yes, she would do that if she could, for all week she had thought again and again of that afternoon and of Ramon's arms holding her safely and securely. Wondrous moments like those would be the things she would want to experience over again.

Glancing in the mirror, she saw that her cheeks were extremely pink and her eyes vividly blue. She looked feverish. She laughed at herself, thinking she looked intoxicated already, even before she had drunk a single glass of wine. Replacing the stopper in the perfume bottle, she began to hum, and swaying her hips as if to the Latin beat of a tango, she crossed to the closet. Surely this night would be eventful and exciting. This was Mexico, and all the songs about the colorful land south of the border said that fiesta was a time of music and romance. Anticipation was making her giddy, she decided, wrinkling her nose and smiling.

She took a turquoise dress with a fitted bodice and a flared skirt from the closet. Putting it on, she smoothed the narrow spaghetti straps over her suntanned shoulders. She smiled with satisfaction. The dress fit her to perfection, accenting the feminine loveliness of her well-proportioned figure. She looked her best and it made her feel happy. Quickly, she clasped a slender strand of cylindrical turquoise beads around her neck. They circled her throat, feeling cool against her warm flesh.

As she left the bedroom and started down the stairs, she glanced down at her feet. She wondered if Ramon would comment on her shoes. He would probably find this pair more ridiculous than those she'd worn in St. Helena, for these were backless, high-heeled wedgies, which were both sexy looking and flattering to her slender feet.

Ramon had been sitting on one of the low couches, reading, but as soon as she appeared he stood up and crossed the room to meet her. He was wearing fawn-colored slacks and a white shirt. She thought she had never seen him look so handsome.

His eyes swept over her in flattering appraisal. *"Muy bonita, señorita.* You'll surely be the most beautiful girl at the fiesta." He let his glance go over her again, this time more slowly, so he took in every detail of her dress, overlooking nothing about her. "I will say, too, that you are more spectacular in that dress than in those jeans and shirts you've been wearing. I approve of every inch of you—including those foolish-looking shoes you're wearing." He smiled and flecks of light sparkled in the dark depths of his eyes. "Though as I recall, I found it difficult to ignore you in your casual apparel." One brow quirked as he took hold of her shoulders and smiled down into her eyes for a moment, before letting his hands slide slowly down her arms. Then he took her hands warmly in his.

His words made her happy, her expectations for the evening ahead rose even higher, and she was flattered by his continued study of her.

"We'll go out to the vineyards shortly, but first I thought you'd like to see your picture in *Renown*," he said, as he led her over to the couch. "They used the shot Dianne took of you standing at the blending table." He picked up the magazine he had been reading and handed it to her.

It was ridiculous, but her hand shook as she took it from him. She looked at the cover. Ramon's profile looked stern, royal, rather like the face of an emperor on a Roman coin. It was impressive, to say the least, set as it was against a montage of scenes of the vineyards. "Ramon, you should be pleased," she said, as she leafed slowly through the pages. "It seems as if at least a fourth of the issue is devoted to Albariza Wines. It's marvelous."

"Ummm," he nodded. "Good publicity, which boosts sales for our wines, is something I'm always glad to have, of course."

She glanced up at him. His face was composed, masklike, revealing nothing of any emotion he might feel. "Did you get this copy today?"

He nodded.

"Did Dianne . . . bring it?" She tried to sound casual as she asked.

"She sent it." He clipped his words off short. "She's not here in Bahía Kino, if that's what you mean."

She pretended to be absorbed in the magazine. "I thought she might have come back for the wine festival." She was careful not to look at Ramon as she spoke. Curiosity nagged at her, for she had a compulsive need to know the depth of his relationship with Dianne. She wanted to learn the answers to her questions without revealing her own feelings to Ramon. She felt so vulnerable where he was concerned.

He smiled enigmatically. "If you want to know if I asked Dianne to come back, the answer is no." His eyes told her that he found her inquisitiveness amusing, but his tone was firm. "I wouldn't want to incur your wrath by performing as less than the ideal host," he continued wryly. "As I recall, the last time I spent an evening with Dianne, you criticized my behavior rather severely."

Gayle could feel her face flush. "For heaven's sake, Ramon, won't you ever forget that?"

He reached out and took the magazine from her. Laying it aside, he held her hands lightly between his. "I'm not sure I *should* forget. After all, you're the first person ever to accuse me of failing to make a guest feel welcome." He studied her face. "I have every intention of correcting that impression." He interlaced his fingers with hers as he spoke.

A warm, intimate feeling of expectancy spiraled through her, and she enjoyed the feeling of being linked to him that the warm pressure of his fingers gave her.

"When *is* Dianne returning, then?"

Ramon's jaw tightened and a muscle twitched along his cheek. "Only Dianne can know the answer to that question. Of course, *Renown* is headquartered in New York, and I do own a vineyard in that state, so perhaps Bahía Kino isn't the only place where we can meet. Who knows? New York is a lovely state, perhaps just the place for a man like me to base his operations."

Gayle's heart skipped a beat. "Are—are you saying you're going to move there?"

"I'm saying that where I live, and how I live, is not a settled thing. And now, if you'll get a shawl for those bare shoulders of yours, we'll go to the fiesta." With those words he dismissed the question of Dianne Bennett.

Once again, as he had done that morning in the

winery, Ramon was letting her know that whatever his relationship with Foster Bennett's daughter happened to be, it was none of her business. Gayle felt the reprimand in his terse words. "I'll get a stole and be right back," she said quietly, and turning away, she moved quickly to the staircase.

The winery glowed with colored lights, yellow and green, blue and red, which were strung along the top of the stucco wall. Large, brightly painted lanterns lighted the plaza area in front of the buildings. At one end of the courtyard, huge barrels of wine were supported on thick wooden braces, and, nearby, long trestle tables covered with vivid red cloths were filled with trays of cheese, baskets of paper thin *tortillas,* loaves of thickly sliced bread and bowls of *guacamole* and *chalupas,* or meat paste. Above this festive scene, the Albariza insignia rippled in the evening breeze.

The sound of guitar music and accordians greeted Gayle and Ramon as eight musicians, wearing colorful serapes and straw sombreros and seated on a small wooden platform, added their melodies to the sounds of clinking glasses and happy voices.

"It sounds as if many of the grape pickers are already well fortified with wine," Ramon said. "I like to see them enjoy themselves." He paused to nod and wave his hand toward Fernando and several of the men from the vineyard. "My people look forward to this occasion; it's a favorite holiday for them. Plenty of food and wine, to which you add women and song, that's the greatest combination for celebration known." He gave her a knowing smile.

"The pickers deserve a treat," she agreed. "I

know how hard they work. It's not an easy job, picking grapes from dawn to dusk. Especially when they have to be handled so carefully, as if they were balls of fragile glass, so they won't be bruised and start fermenting." She paused, suddenly feeling foolish. After all, he knew far more about the process than she did, yet here she was, telling him what of course he already knew.

"They work hard, and as you can see tonight, they play hard." Laughing, he circled her waist with his arm, keeping her close at his side. The workers began gathering around, clustering close to Ramon. "They're waiting for me to make the celebration official," he said, bending his head close to her ear. Together, they walked to the musicians' platform and Ramon stepped up on it, indicating to Gayle that she should stand nearby where he could look down at her.

A smiling Fernando marched through the crowd toward Ramon and the people stepped aside to make way for him. He was carrying a tall bottle in one hand and a clean wine glass in the other, holding both above his head as he walked. When he was standing directly in front of Ramon, he handed him first the glass, then, uncorking the bottle with a flourish, passed it to him as well. Ramon filled the glass a quarter full with the new wine and lifted it in salute to the crowd around him.

"Amigos," he said loudly, the strong planes of his face lifted in a smile, "We shall all drink of the best of all wines—ALBARIZA WINES!" Then he repeated the words in Spanish. Loud clapping and the cheers of the workers saluted his words. Ramon then drained his glass and, refilling it, jumped from the platform and handed it to Fernando. A grin split

the stocky Mexican's face and he drank the wine and proceeded to fill the glass again and pass it on to a fellow worker.

Gayle watched the ceremony, fascinated. The glass of wine was passed to each man in turn, and each felt honored when it was his turn to hold it in his hand and raise it to his lips. Gayle found it fascinating, for she had already learned from Maria what an important part tradition played in the lives of those who worked for Ramon and Albariza Wines.

"You enjoyed this?" Gayle felt Ramon's arm around her shoulder.

"I think it's glorious," she cried.

He laughed at her excited tone. "Come on, then. We must officially open the dancing as well as the wine tasting." He lifted his hand to signal the musicians and they began playing again. The music was rhythmic and vivid, and though Gayle found the tune unfamiliar, it was vibrant and catchy and she found herself humming along. She thought of her father and Golden Valley. The celebration following the grape harvest in the Napa Valley could never match this. She sighed, feeling a mixture of both contentment and excitement at being a part of this extraordinary scene.

"*Señorita,* we shall dance," Ramon announced, and as he drew her close in his arms, all thought of the Napa Valley or anything but the pressure of his hand on her back vanished from her thoughts. He led her expertly into the Latin rhythm of the music. "We dance well together, Gayle," he said, his warm breath touching her face. "But then, I knew we would." He drew her closer, fitting her body to his.

Her blood ran like fire along her veins and her

body betrayed her with every breath she took and every movement that she made. She faltered, missing a step. Pressed close to him like this, the hypnotic rhythm of his body was having a disturbing effect on her senses. As if he understood her emotional response to him, he brushed his lips across her temple and, with a light touch on her spine, communicated a caressing instruction to relax. She could feel herself becoming involuntarily soft and pliable in his arms.

The guitars now drifted into a slower and more melodic piece. The provocative sounds were almost too lovely, and a rapturous sensuousness engulfed her. As Ramon's breathing stirred the hair that curled softly against her cheek, she inhaled the sweet, intoxicating smell of the new wine he had tasted. She was filled with an indisputable awareness of her love for this man.

Struggling to control her undisciplined emotions, she attempted to ease herself slightly within the close confines of his arms.

"That's a—a beautiful melody. What is it?" She had difficulty speaking, so affected was she by his nearness.

Ramon brushed his lips across her cheek again as he moved his face from hers and looked into her eyes. "It's called *Querida Mia*," he answered, his low voice accenting the Spanish words in that soft, slurring tone of his.

"What does that mean?" She felt hesitant, wanting to know, but almost afraid to hear the translation. For she remembered that he had called her *"querida"* on the beach that day.

A flicker of emotion stirred in the depths of his eyes. "It means 'my darling' or 'my beloved one.'"

She trembled, feeling a breathless sense of elation. Could Ramon possibly have meant the endearment? Or had he said those words only to soothe her because she was so terrified by the Seri? *"Querida mia,"* she repeated the words softly. "It has a lovely sound." Lowering her eyes, she kept from looking at him.

"The music?" he questioned.

She knew he was studying her face, she could feel it as surely as if he were tracing her eyes, her nose and her lips with his finger. Flushing under his gaze, she stole a look at him through her lowered lashes. "The music, of course, but I actually meant the sound of the Spanish words." Her face grew warmer. She was embarrassed to be carrying on so over the title of a song.

If he found her conversation inane, he gave no evidence of it. Instead, he pulled her close again and put his cool cheek against her flushed one. "When this dance is over I want to take you into the winery. I've something to show you. I have a surprise for you." Ramon's mouth was close to her ear and there was an intimate quality in his voice that made her heart beat erratically.

"What kind of surprise?" Perhaps it was all due to the romantic aura of the fiesta, but she felt exhilarated and filled with an expectancy that made her breathless.

"One I very much hope will please you, and . . ." He hesitated. Then, without finishing whatever it was he had started to say, he moved her with two long, gliding steps away from the area in front of the guitar players. Letting go of her hand, he turned her so she walked beside him. He still kept his arm around her, his hand resting on her back just above her waist. Its guiding pressure was light, but sufficient for her to be aware of the contact and be strangely unnerved by it. It seemed that in the past few minutes all her nerves and senses had become vibrantly alive and glowing because of the powerful attraction Ramon held for her. Suddenly life held new promise, for it seemed that he might feel something for her after all.

They entered the winery and their steps matched as the two of them moved down the hall to the blending room. "I had planned to save my surprise until the end of the fiesta, to make it the climax of the evening." He smiled and lengthened his stride, pulling her along with him.

"I'm glad you didn't make me wait. Once you told me about it, I'd have died if I couldn't know right away what it was." She laughed up at him. "Patience is not one of my virtues."

"Nor one of mine." He stopped, suddenly, and turned her into his arms. "And I'm not waiting another second to kiss you, either."

Before his words touched her ears, his mouth claimed hers and he kissed her deeply, lingeringly, in a way that sent her senses spinning. When he finally moved his face from hers, he looked at her for a long moment. His eyes held hers with a searching intensity that seemed to seek and probe the depths of her emotions.

"You're beautiful—golden and beautiful," he said huskily. "And you're more intoxicating than any wine." His voice was low and she barely heard it because of the pounding in her ears. The words pulsated in her head as if he were repeating them to her. "More intoxicating than any wine." As he had said the words, she had, for one breathless moment, felt his desire for her move rampant through his whip-lean body. She longed to respond, to cling to him, but she forced herself to stand away from him and hold her body straight and refrain from touching him. It was all just the spell of this night of fiesta. Wasn't it? She felt that, if it was, her heart would surely break.

His look was unfathomable as he let her move away. Opening the door to the blending room, he stepped aside to allow her to enter. "Go in, Gayle, and let me show you my surprise." He touched her elbow and walked with her to the blending table where all the sample bottles were neatly aligned. Taking a clean glass, he poured wine from one of the bottles. "The first of next week, we will begin to bottle the sherry," he said. Gayle recognized the pride, the ring of triumph, in his voice. "It will never surpass my grandfather's sherry, but it may well equal it. I believe it will prove to be the finest produced anywhere outside of Spain."

"Oh, Ramon . . . I know what this must mean to you."

His smile deepened the creases on either side of his mouth, mirroring the satisfaction he felt. "I think, perhaps, you do." His fingers smoothed the stem of the wine glass with a caress that was almost sensuous. Gayle thought of the strength of Ramon's hands, knowing he could snap the stem with only the slightest pressure. Yet his fingers touched the glass of this wine he had labored so long to develop as a lover would stroke his cherished bride.

His fingers brushed hers as he placed the glass in her hand. "Taste it, *por favor,*" he said solemnly.

Her heartbeat accelerated and she felt an empathy

with him. "The color is flawless," she said, holding the glass up to the light. She was conscious of the intensity with which he watched her, as if her reactions were important to him. She lifted the wine to her lips and slowly tasted it, closing her eyes to concentrate on the flavor. As she opened her eyes, her lips parted in a sigh. "It's superb; the excellence you were seeking is there."

Ramon nodded. *"Sí."* He smiled at her. "It is all I hoped for. And because it is, I wanted a name, a label, that would embody both its perfection and its tradition." He took the glass from her hand and set it down on the blending table. "Perfection is the warm amber beauty like yours." He touched her hair where it curled softly over her ears.

Her breath caught in her throat at his words. He trailed his hand gently across her cheek before reaching into his pocket and pulling out a square of paper. "This is the label for the finest wine I have ever made." He held the paper in the palm of his hand for her to see.

Gayle gasped as she beheld the rich, royal blue label with the impressive gilt lettering which spelled out the name of the wine—ALBARIZA AMBER. Her eyes grew luminous with tears which made the golden elegance of the letters blur in her vision. "Albariza Amber," she whispered, her lips forming the words almost soundlessly.

"It says it all. Don't you agree?" He was looking at her as if he couldn't get enough of the sight, as if her reaction to the label was exactly as he had wanted it to be.

The floor seemed to rock beneath her feet and she swayed toward him. He caught her shoulders and pulled her hard against him, and his mouth came down on hers with a hungry passion that overpowered her. His hands were warm and caressing on her shoulders; he pushed aside the narrow straps of her dress and his fingers moved from her shoulders to the creamy softness of her throat. Her heart was racing and she felt boneless, hardly able to stand.

The hands that had been subtly caressing now moved over her with a mounting eagerness. She clung to him, overcome by a surge of feeling that impelled a heated response from her lips and left her body weak and melting with desire. She raised her arms, placing them around his neck, molding herself even closer to him. She could feel his heart beat wildly against her breast and their lips met again with a fierce urgency as his arms pressed tightly around her yielding body.

"Let's get out of here, Gayle," he said thickly, drawing his mouth reluctantly from hers. And as he looked at her, the blazing passion in his eyes jolted through her. "We can't stay here. You know that, don't you?" A smile touched his mouth with sensual warmth, the sight of which made her heart turn over, and she felt her blood leap in response to his implied question.

"Ramon, I . . ."

He put his finger gently on her lips. "Don't say anything now." Taking her hand, he drew her through the door and they fled down the corridor. As they rushed out of the building, Ramon bent his head close to hers. "We'll march through the crowd and out the gate to my car. No one will even know we're gone." He winked at her, and at the same time possessively circled her waist with his arm.

"I don't think I should take the host away from his own party," she teased. "Maybe we should stay until the *fiesta* is over." She slowed her steps as if to halt their escape.

"No, my enticing amber witch. You and I are leaving right now!" He pulled her closer, forcing her steps to keep up with his. Laughing up at him, she nodded her head in consent. Happiness welled inside her. She didn't mind at all that he had called her an amber witch. This time, the way he had looked at her and the tone of his voice, had made it sound like a term of impassioned endearment. They walked rapidly toward the gate. Gayle's thoughts were all for her indisputable awareness of the depth of her love for Ramon. She was scarcely conscious of anything but her emotions and the feeling of his body brushing against her as they moved.

"Ramon! Gayle! Wait for me!" The sound of someone calling out to them startled her. She stumbled forward and might have fallen, except for Ramon's arm around her, supporting her. "Ramon, Gayle, please wait." Hearing their names again, they turned to see Carmelita running to catch up to them. "I have to see you. I must talk to you, Ramon! Right now!" Her voice rang with excitement and she reached out for Ramon's arm to detain him.

Gayle was struck again by Carmelita's incandescent beauty. Gayle had never seen her look more vibrant than she did at this moment. Her pastel yellow dress set off her dark hair and flawless skin, while her eyes were deep and tawny and completely enchanting.

"It's Juan, I have to tell you about Juan. You must listen to me!" Her voice rose with each excited word.

"Oh, Ramon—Juan has this marvelous opportunity to buy another shrimp boat. It's so important to him and I want to help him. Why, if he had two boats, he could be the most prosperous shrimper on the bay. He'd have the largest catch night after night." She ran her words together in her jubilation.

"Carmelita, be still a moment, *por favor.*" Ramon laughed at her wild enthusiasm. "You sound as if you've already had too much wine, and the evening has just begun," he teased her good-naturedly.

"No, no. I haven't had even a single glass." She stamped her foot impatiently. "You never pay attention to me, Ramon. Please, you must listen to me this time." She pouted prettily. "Please, this is so important to me."

"*Sí, chiquita,*" He nodded, giving her a tolerant smile. "*Sí;* I'm listening."

"I've made an important decision." She straightened, standing as tall as her petite height would allow. Tilting her head back, she looked determinedly up into Ramon's face. "I'm not going to the university, Ramon. Instead, I want to give my college money to Juan so he can buy this second boat."

Ramon stared at her in astonishment. "Of course you're going to the university. Don't talk like an absurd little fool." He rubbed his hand across his chin, his eyes narrowing and never leaving the Mexican girl's face. Dropping his arm from Gayle's waist, it seemed as if he had forgotten about her. Indeed, it now appeared clear that she had no part at all in this drama unfolding between Ramon and Carmelita.

"I am not going. I want to help Juan." The girl's voice throbbed with emotion. "I don't care about

college. That was all your idea anyway, Ramon."
Her words now were edged with youthful rebellion.

"You damn well better care!" A muscle jerked in
the side of Ramon's jaw as he clenched his teeth
over his words. "You must finish your education,
Carmelita. It is vital for you."

"What is vital to me is to help Juan." Her voice
rose in defiance. "Why do I need four years at the
university?"

Ramon's dark eyes flashed with anger. "You know
all too well what you need and why." His voice held
a frightening coldness. "You're not a poverty-
stricken nobody. Remember that, Carmelita. You
have Maria and Fernando to consider."

The pretty girl flung her dark head high and
looked squarely at Ramon, her eyes luminous with
tears. "It doesn't matter to me—none of it. I've
made my decision." There was stony determination
underlining her words.

Gayle felt herself cringe as she stepped backward
to escape the tension that electrified the air between
these two. The clash of their wills was disturbing to
her in ways she couldn't name.

"You will go as planned to Monterrey tomorrow
and you will attend the university. That's how it is to
be and I don't want to hear another word of anything
else." Ramon sounded like a general issuing an
order to a subordinate who could not possibly question his authority. It seemed, however, that Carmelita intended to have the last word.

The girl's lips trembled, but still she stood in front
of Ramon, her small frame rigid. "I shall not go. If
you won't allow me to give Juan my college money,
then I'll find another way to help him." She wiped
the tears of frustration from her eyes. "I know you

feel you are doing what is best for me, but you are wrong, Ramon." There was a quiet dignity to the girl's manner and voice. "You see, I love Juan, and I'm going to stay here and marry him."

Ramon's face flamed with rage at Carmelita's words. "Marry Juan! Don't be a fool! You're too young and immature to marry anyone," he yelled at her, lifting his hand in angry protest.

Gayle stared in horror. Surely he was not going to slap Fernando's daughter? "Stop it, Ramon," she cried, as she stepped between them.

Carmelita crossed her arms over her breasts as if to shield herself, but she did not back away. Ramon grabbed Gayle by the shoulders, shoving her aside. "Stay out of this, Gayle. It has nothing to do with you." His tone was harsh and his face was like granite. "Go get some wine and leave us alone for a minute." He brushed her aside as if she were an unwanted obstruction. Then he reached out for Carmelita, taking hold of her arm. "We're going inside." He drew her back toward the door of the building. "We must settle this, Carmelita, and in an intelligent way that considers everyone involved," he said firmly.

Gayle didn't wait to hear more, for Ramon had, in effect, banished her from the scene. She walked away from them into the crowd that clustered near the costumed musicians. Moving as rapidly as she could, she stumbled against a reveler with a glass of wine in his hand, causing him to tip his glass and splash red wine on the skirt of her dress. She paid no heed, did not attempt to wipe it away. She simply did not care. It no longer mattered that she had worn her prettiest dress tonight or that she had wanted to look beautiful for the fiesta. She had wanted Ramon to admire her, to find her attractive and desirable. And he had, but it was of no importance now.

Pushing through the crowd, she hurried faster, and by the time she reached the stucco wall that surrounded the plaza, she had broken into a run. She fled through the iron gates and, once outside and away from the people, she leaned against the wall. Covering her face with trembling hands, she breathed the night air in breathless gasps that wracked her chest like painful sobs.

How humiliated she felt. How could she have been so stupid, so foolish, as to believe for a moment that Ramon could truly care for her? Just because he had flattered her with his soft, slurring voice, told her she was beautiful, like his precious amber wine. What a romantic fool she was to be so taken in by his seductive words and persuasive kisses. She had been insane to think even for a minute that he loved her simply because he had held her intimately in his arms, because he told her the meaning of the words *"querida mia."* A strangled, anguished laugh tore from her throat. She must be a madwoman to hope, even for a single moment, that Ramon could ever make *her* his beloved one.

She rubbed her hand across her eyes. How blind she had been. But she could see all too clearly now. She herself was nothing more than a pleasant diversion. Even Dianne was no more than a brief amusement. It was Carmelita he loved. The beautiful Mexican girl was the one Ramon really cared for. Why else would he have arranged for her education? He had been planning all along to groom her to take her place beside him as mistress of Casa del Mar. No wonder he didn't want her to marry Juan. He wanted Carmelita for himself—and why not? She was the perfect choice. A dark, sultry, Mexican *señorita* who belonged here in Bahía Kino. She had even been raised in the Albariza vineyards.

Gayle could feel her temples throbbing. Pressing her forehead with her fingers, she rubbed them with a circular motion. An odd thought moved in her mind. She doubted if Ramon had even admitted his feeling for Carmelita to himself before tonight. All this time he had been making plans for her education and training and simply waiting for her to mature, to grow and become the woman he was seeking. After tonight, he would have to admit how deeply he cared, because why else would he have become so enraged because she wanted to help Juan, and because she thought she loved the young fisherman? Ramon's jealousy had brought about the whole ugly scene. He had hurled his wrath in Carmelita's pretty face because he could not tolerate the thought that she would prefer a mere shrimp boat owner to him. A bitter smile twisted the corners of Gayle's mouth.

Moving away from the support of the wall, she straightened her shoulders and walked back through the iron gates. She must see if she could find Fernando and ask him to drive her back to the *casa*. Surely he wouldn't mind. It would take him only about twenty minutes and he could get right back to the festival. She knew she had to leave, and the sooner the better. Certainly she did not want to have to see Ramon again tonight, nor did she want to hear the music or drink the wine. As far as she was concerned, the fiesta was over—in fact, for her, the spell of enchantment that Mexico had cast upon her was now broken, ended once and for all.

Chapter Nine

Gayle did not know how long she had remained outside, absorbed in her painful thoughts. It must have been quite some time, however, for the gaiety of the people inside had reached a high pitch. Obviously, a good deal of the new wine had been consumed by the many celebrants. Gayle mingled with the vineyard workers, trying to catch sight of Fernando and Maria. She moved from one laughing, high-spirited group to the next, but neither of them seemed to be anywhere around the courtyard. Perhaps Ramon had summoned them to the winery to enlist their help with Carmelita. Having no wish to risk seeing Ramon again, she dismissed the thought of looking for Fernando inside the building. She frowned, realizing she would simply have to be patient and wait.

Wandering over to the harvest table, she picked up a narrow wedge of cheese and nibbled on it.

Taking two crackers in her other hand, she walked to where one of the young men was filling bottles with red wine from one of the huge barrels, having now decided she would have a glass of wine after all. When the young Mexican had filled her glass, she returned to the table and ladled *chalupas* onto a crisply fried *tortilla*.

During the next half hour or more, many of the Mexicans she knew from the winery came around to speak to her and introduce their wives and girl friends. Gayle wished her Spanish vocabulary were not so limited, so she could converse more easily with these friendly couples. Fortunately, everyone's festive mood made for an easy rapport without an abundance of words.

Gayle contemplated having another glass of wine, for it did seem she was stuck here at the fiesta whether she wished it or not. Her head still ached slightly, but either the friendliness of the vineyard people or the food she had eaten had somehow made her feel better, and perhaps more wine would dissolve the remaining bitter edges of her tension.

There was a lull in the revelry as the musicians took an intermission and descended on the food. Their performance had apparently stimulated their appetites, for they partook of the food and wine voraciously.

Gayle's attention was suddenly arrested and her gaze shot upward as the blinding flash of strobe lights shattered the darkness overhead. The sound of screaming engines pierced her ears as a low flying plane ripped open the night sky with its passing. Gayle stood transfixed, paralyzed by the realization that it had to be Ramon's plane. Why was he flying away from the vineyard so late at night? Where

could he be going? And who was in the plane with
him? Still unmoving, she stared now into the silent
emptiness, for Ramon's plane had disappeared,
swallowed up into the black hole of the night. . . .

A short time later, Gayle saw Fernando and Maria
coming through the front gates, returning to the
fiesta from wherever they had been. She waved to
them and they came over and joined her near the
harvest table.

"Ramon looked for you before he left," Maria
said. "He asked us to tell you to excuse him, but he
had to take Carmelita to Monterrey." The Mexican
woman spoke quietly and her face looked pinched
and tired.

Fernando hunched his heavy shoulders in a shrug
of resignation. "It was best that he got that foolish
girl to the university without any further delay."

It was all settled, then, Gayle thought. The master
of the vineyards had manipulated the impetuous
Carmelita into doing his bidding after all.

"It's my fault. I should have forbidden her to see
so much of Juan." Maria shook her head in remorse.

"No, the blame is not yours." Fernando put his
arm around his wife. "Nothing either of us could
have done would have stopped our fiery Carmelita.
You know how she is." He shook his head and gave
Maria a reassuring pat. "It is best to let Ramon
handle her."

Maria bristled with anger. "Ramon is always the
one who must do everything. You're too easygoing,
Fernando," she scolded. "You've let Carmelita have
her own way so often that no wonder she is so hard
to manage." Her voice grew louder as she re-
proached him.

The round-faced Mexican smiled good-naturedly.

"No real harm has been done, and Ramon has taken care of everything." He turned toward Gayle. "The only problem is that I fear the fiesta has been spoiled for you, *señorita.*"

"Yes, and look what has happened to your lovely dress," Maria said with characteristic concern.

"It's only a little wine and maybe it won't stain." Gayle tried to make light of the mishap. "I am tired, however." She rubbed her head; she could feel her headache returning. "If you two don't mind, I'd like very much to return to the *casa.*"

Maria agreed quickly and Fernando nodded his head at the two of them. "Ramon instructed me to pay the musicians. I'll do that right now and then we will go." He hurried off in the direction of the platform, where the men had returned to their guitars and accordians but were now playing in a more comfortable and relaxed fashion, having discarded their sombreros.

It was after midnight when they returned to the *casa.* Gayle said good night to Maria and Fernando and went directly upstairs to her room. She did have several things left to settle in her mind, but one thing she was certain of. She would pack tomorrow, Sunday, so as to be ready to leave the first thing on Monday. She could hardly ask Fernando to drive her to Hermosillo on Sunday, and the public bus was unpredictable most days, and particularly so on the weekends. It would be especially so tomorrow, following such an extensive celebration of the harvest. The thought made her smile, for tomorrow everyone would either be sleeping off the effects of so much wine or saying penance at the old mission church for tonight's revelry. She would leave on

Monday, then, and that would be convenient for Fernando as well. Anything was fine just as long as she left Casa del Mar before Ramon returned.

The following morning she stayed in her room until she was certain Maria and Fernando would have left for Mass. Maria had left a fresh pot of coffee for her and a slice of cantaloupe was carefully covered and chilling in the refrigerator. After eating the melon and having a piece of toast with her coffee, she carried a second cup of coffee back upstairs so she could drink it as she packed.

Taking clothes from the closet she folded them on the bed, ready to lay in her large suitcase. She had had the cotton shift Ramon had given her laundered fresh each day, and she had worn one of her own gowns last night. Now she folded the soft cotton garment which had belonged to Ramon's mother into a neat square and carried it over to the highboy. Opening the bottom drawer, she laid it carefully inside. The drawer was full, so she smoothed her hands over the top, pressing the contents down flat so the drawer would close again easily. She felt a solid object underneath the layers of cloth that felt as if it could be a rectangular tray. Curious, she lifted the top items and discovered an oil painting in an ornate, gold-leaf frame. It was the portrait of a beautiful young woman. Gayle stared at the canvas, fascinated by the dusky, violet eyes which were the most striking feature of the perfectly proportioned face. The porcelain quality of the skin and the amber-gold hair told Gayle that the portrait was of Ramon's mother. How truly beautiful she had been. Even the look of sadness the artist had captured in her eyes did not lessen the compelling beauty of the face. Narrowing her eyes, she peered at the signature in the left hand corner of the canvas: Esteban Valdez. Her eyes flared. Esteban Valdez was a widely renowned, twentieth-century Mexican artist. Why, his work had even been compared to that of the great Spanish artist, Goya. Ramon should have this painting hanging in the living room, not buried in the bottom drawer of a chest.

She sighed. She was depressed enough this morning. Why must everything she did bring Ramon right back into her thoughts again? She had to push him from her mind. She had to leave this house. She closed her eyes for a moment and pressed her lips tightly together. When would she stop being such a fool? Would she ever become wise enough to love someone who could love her in return?

"Excuse me, *señorita*. I wanted to let you know we're back and—" Maria's voice stopped in surprise and she stood in the doorway, gaping at Gayle. "You—you cannot be packing your suitcase? *Señor-ita*, what has happened? What is wrong?" She scurried across the room like a concerned mother hen.

Gayle could feel herself flush, disconcerted by Maria's sudden appearance. "Nothing is wrong. I mean, I *am* packing, but—" She spoke hesitantly, she was so flustered. She knew she must find some excuse to give Maria. "I find I need to go back to California tomorrow. I must see my father."

"*Qué lástima*, what a pity. Señor Ramon will be distressed to learn you are leaving."

Gayle turned away from Maria's concerned gaze. The Mexican woman was very perceptive. She must be careful not to reveal the turmoil she was in because of Carmelita. "I—I was putting away the cotton gown and I discovered this lovely painting," she hastened to change the subject, but at the same time she didn't want Maria to think she had been probing through Señora Louise's personal things. "I couldn't resist admiring it. The artist, Esteban Valdez, is very well-known, very fine." She spoke rapidly, trying to hide her emotional state behind a profusion of words.

"*Sí*, I have been told so. He is dead now." There was an almost imperceptible hint of enmity in her voice.

"Maria, why is this portrait not on display in the *casa?*" She asked the question almost involuntarily.

The housekeeper's dark eyes were sober. "For a time it was." She shook her head sadly. "But the day after the *señor* and *señora* were killed, Ramon instructed me to take it down and put it out of sight—and I did."

Gayle drew her breath in sharply. "It wasn't only because of his sorrow over their tragic death though, was it?" She felt somehow compelled to ask this question.

"No, *señorita*—it was because he blamed his mother for his father's death." Lines of sorrow now etched her face.

"Blamed her? Oh, Maria, how could that be? I knew Ramon felt some bitterness toward his mother, but from what he's told me, I thought it was because she didn't like the vineyards, that she was lonely and unhappy here. He does seem to resent the fact that she left for long periods of time. But Fernando told me they died in a plane crash. How was that her fault?"

"The *señora* was away from the *casa* many months at a time." She paused, and smoothed the skirt of her dress with quick, nervous movements. "I think

167

perhaps Ramon would not like it that I discuss his family with you." She looked intently into Gayle's face, her lips pursed thoughtfully. "I would like you to understand about Señora Louise, however, for she was a very great, very sad woman. She was too beautiful and too sensitive." She looked at the portrait Gayle still held in her hands. "She wanted a constant show of attention from those around her, she needed the assurance that she was loved and admired. Since the *señor* was starting the vineyards here in Mexico, perhaps he gave his work too much of his time and energy."

"This lovely house, Casa del Mar, surely she was happy to have such a beautiful home, and a child?"

"Those early years were happy ones. She was busy taking care of Ramon and she was, if anything, too devoted a mother. Once Ramon was sent away to school, everything changed. The schools were not much good here, for this is a poor area of Mexico, and the *señor* insisted Ramon go to a private school in Guadalajara." Maria's voice softened, and she seemed to be lost in reminiscing, for her eyes held a faraway look with a trace of melancholy. "For a time, I think she was very angry at Ramon's father for sending the boy to Guadalajara. After that, she grew bored, and began to go off to Mexico City four or five times a year. Before long, she spent more time there than here in Bahía Kino."

"Why didn't Ramon's father stop her? Why did he let her go for such long periods."

"He wanted her to enjoy life and be happy. There was no social life for her here, and she had the theaters and art galleries and activities that contented her there."

Gayle narrowed her eyes in a frown. "But none of

this explains why Ramon blames his mother for the plane crash."

"Señora Louise fell in love with Esteban Valdez and they were lovers until he died," Maria said, and took the portrait from Gayle and knelt down to replace it in the open drawer of the highboy. "She kept this from Ramon's father all through the years. I was the only one who knew, and that was only because she was ill one fall in Mexico City and she asked me to come and take care of her. It was grape harvest, and she insisted that Señor Arnoldo must stay here and see to the wine, so I went alone, and learned about her affair." She closed the drawer and stood up. "If it had not been for the will left by Valdez, I think perhaps the *señor* might never have learned about it." She told Gayle all of this in quiet, unemotional words.

Gayle's expression was doubting. "You can't mean that Esteban Valdez spelled out their relationship in his will?"

"Not in words, but he did leave three extremely valuable paintings to her, and Señor Arnoldo asked her to explain why she should inherit such costly works and she told him."

"Was this just before the plane crash? I mean, does Ramon blame his mother for revealing the truth to his father?"

"I don't know Ramon's feelings for certain, of course. But I do know what happened in this house when Señor Arnoldo learned the facts of Valdez's will. He ordered the *señora* to donate the paintings to the museum in Mexico City, for he felt if she did, she would appear as a patron of the arts and escape having undue notice made of the fact that the artist had left the paintings to her." Maria's face was

169

drawn in tight lines. "The *señor* was a man of great pride, and I believe he would have done almost anything to keep shame and scandal from marring the name of Albariza."

"Then the paintings were given to the museum?"

Maria shook her head. "Señora Louise would not hear of it. She begged and pleaded with Ramon's father to let her keep the paintings, and finally he agreed to fly her to Mexico City to collect them, and it was when they were returning that the accident occurred."

Gayle could see tears in the kind woman's dark eyes. "What a tragedy for Ramon, to lose both his parents at the same time, and under ugly circumstances," she said quietly, gently touching Maria's arm.

Maria put a thin brown hand on top of Gayle's. "Ramon never said it to me, but he told Fernando that he knew his father deliberately crashed the plane into the sea that night. His father knew every part of this area like his own face. He could never have mistaken the little bird island for the vineyards, no matter how dark and moonless the night." She sighed, and her lips trembled. "We will not speak again of this," she said, as she composed herself by straightening her shoulders and once again smoothing the fullness of her skirt. "Now, if you really must leave tomorrow, would you like me to help you pack? Or shall I go see about lunch?"

"Please, you go ahead with lunch. It won't take me long to pack; I'll be through in half an hour or less." Gayle managed to smile thinly. She was still thinking of what Maria had just told her. It was not a pleasant story, but it did go a long way to explain Ramon's attitude toward American women. "I'll come down as soon as I finish here," she added quickly, as Maria left the room.

When she had almost finished packing, she picked up the ironwood carving from the dresser. Tears blurred her vision as she looked at the graceful pelican with his remarkable beak. She would miss everything here, the sights and sounds of the sea, this lovely house, her work at the vineyards—and Ramon. "Oh, Ramon," she whispered his name. If only he could have loved her. Her lashes were wet now, and she blinked back tears and held the carving firmly. She thought that never before had she felt as she did now—hollow, empty. Slowly, she walked across the room to where her suitcase lay open on top of the bed. Carefully, she surrounded the carving with soft articles of clothing. Then, closing the lid, she snapped the locks shut and turned away, walking out of the blue bedroom and down the stairs to join Maria and Fernando for lunch.

Chapter Ten

"Gayle," Fernando said after lunch, "if you must leave Bahía Kino tomorrow, let me take you over to the pelican island later this afternoon."

"I don't want to interrupt your Sunday. Thank you, though." She smiled, and stood up to clear the table for Maria. She appreciated how thoughtful both of them had been to her from the first day she arrived in Mexico.

"You did ask me if you could see the island and I promised, remember?" Fernando's familiar grin spread warmly across his broad face.

"I would like to see it, of course. I just hate for you to go to the trouble."

"No problem, *señorita*. It takes less than ten minutes to run over there in the motorboat. The sun is too hot now, but by about three o'clock it will be lower, and the island itself has a good deal of shade."

The prospect lifted her spirits. She was grateful for the opportunity to see the island and, in fact, welcomed any activity that might divert her and banish the painful thoughts that plagued her.

The ocean swelled as the small motor launch headed away from the white sandy beach in front of the *casa* and headed toward the open sea. The island, called Alcatraz by the Mexicans, looked like a green hill rising from the sea, like a humpbacked piece of green jade. It was farther from the mainland than it looked, and though Fernando had said the trip would take only ten minutes, it actually was closer to twenty-five before they reached the edge of the island, where a narrow, curving beach of white sand edged a sea of translucent green.

She had thought they would only spend a brief time viewing the island, so she was pleased when Fernando told her he would leave her there to explore and then return to pick her up before sunset. Before he left, he pointed out to her how all the paths on the island went from the beach inward to the center, like the spokes of a wheel, the hub of which was the *cabaña* built for Ramon's mother. Fernando handed her a key. "This will unlock the door for you, Gayle, and after you've explored the surroundings, I know you will enjoy the *cabaña*. I'll leave this thermos of drinking water here by this tree for you, but you will also find cans of fruit juice and soda in the hut." He climbed back aboard the boat and, after a quick wave, he started the motor and the boat sped away, churning the water into white waves in its wake.

Gayle took her time, walking along the narrow footpaths that marked the area into pie-shaped wedges. Though the base of the island appeared to be mostly rock, there was enough soil to nurture shrubs and low trees, whose sprawling, umbrellalike branches provided cool shade. The rumble of the surf against the wet rocks was a pleasant growl which she found soothing as she walked where the low branches of the trees met above her head. It was like moving through a green tunnel, the leaves blocking out her view of the sky. She thought she heard an airplane, but decided it was only her subconscious mind recalling Ramon's plane flying away the night before.

After she had explored all the outer areas of the island, she turned toward the center, following a gradual incline that led to a clearing where the small *cabaña* stood, its white adobe walls crowned by a red tile roof. Unlocking the black arched door with the key Fernando had given her, she stepped inside the cool interior. The room was murky and shadowed. Gayle walked around, pushing open the shutters that covered the long windows at the sides and back of the room. The late afternoon sunlight filtered wanly into the white-walled room, disclosing the rusty red of the unglazed tiles which covered the floor. The furnishings were few, but charming in their simple decorativeness. A wrought-iron pedestal table with a plate-glass top was surrounded by four chairs of white painted metal with blue- and green-striped cushioned seats. Under the long windows on each of the side walls were built-in window seats, which were cushioned with thick pads covered in the same striped fabric as the chair seats. These seemed to serve as couches for relaxing or as beds for sleeping, in the event that someone should want to stay on the island overnight. The back wall held a tall cupboard.

Gayle opened the double wooden doors and viewed the shelves, neatly covered with a set of Mexican pottery dishes and a half-dozen drinking glasses. The lower shelves held emergency rations: canned foods, fruit juices and soft drinks. In addition, six bottles of Albariza wine were placed horizontally along the bottom shelf. She smiled at the sight of the wine. One might not manage a very exciting meal from the supply of canned goods, but there was certainly sufficient wine to wash it down.

Having completed her inspection of the provisions, she sat down on one of the window seats, leaning her back against the wall. The rough adobe brick felt cool, even damp, through the thin material of her blouse. Reaching to the corner of the seat, she tugged gently to ease a pillow from under the stack of folded Mexican blankets so she could use it to cushion her back. She was so intent on freeing the pillow without knocking any of the blankets onto the floor that she didn't hear the door open.

"Let me get that for you." Ramon's low voice penetrated the stillness of the room.

Startled, she flung her head back, bumping it sharply against the wall. Her strangled cry of pain mixed with fright was shrill.

"Gayle, I'm sorry. I didn't mean to frighten you." He crossed to her in three long strides and sat down close beside her, putting his hand to the back of her head. "I bet you gave yourself a goose egg." He rubbed her hair gently as he spoke.

"I'm sure I didn't crack it that hard." Her words were breathy. It was upsetting enough to have him appear so unexpectedly, but his touch totally unnerved her. "What—what are you doing here?" She managed to move away from him and she turned on the seat so that her knees formed a barrier between them.

Amusement flickered across his face at her almost frenzied attempts to put some distance between them. "I'm here looking for you. Surely you must have known I would be." His eyes held question marks that disappeared as he smiled teasingly. "Now, come close to me, where I can touch you as we talk." Putting his hands on her knees, he pushed gently to move her legs out of the way.

"Don't, Ramon." She pressed her legs firmly into the padded seat. "It's better we talk this way."

He was eyeing her intently now, and there was no longer even a trace of good humor in his expression. "When I got back from Monterrey, less than an hour ago, Fernando met me with some wild story that you're leaving tomorrow. That's preposterous—you know that!"

Gayle pressed her hands together in her lap and didn't say anything.

"I thought last night that you and I . . ." He leaned toward her. "Damn it, Gayle, I can't believe you were using me again. What more proof do you require? You know what a beautiful, desirable woman you are. I want you—need you. You know that I do! Why would you even suggest leaving here now?"

His penetrating eyes had a disturbing power over her. "I—I have to," she stammered. "I realize, now, that it's the best thing for me to do." She was struggling to make her words sound matter-of-fact and keep her emotions under control.

"Why?" he demanded.

"Because . . ."

"'Because' is not an answer." He reached over and put his thumb under her chin, tilting her face so she was forced to look at him. "Is something wrong that I don't know about?" He scrutinized her with his dark, piercing eyes. "Did Maria or Fernando upset you?"

"No, of course not." She shook her head sharply, not only to emphasize her words, but to escape the touch of his fingers on her face. "The two of them have been marvelous to me since the moment I arrived."

"And I haven't? Is that what you're implying?" He covered her clenched hands where they lay in her lap and rubbed the tips of her fingers with his. "Are you scolding me again for being a poor host?"

She dislodged her hands from his. "Don't be ridiculous." Her voice shook, revealing how aware she had been of the subtle pressure of his hands on hers. "Really, Ramon, since you didn't want me here in the first place, I thought you'd be relieved to have me leave."

"Well, I'm not. Furthermore, I have no intention of letting you go. You made a bargain with me to work in my vineyards and learn winemaking, and I have a good deal more to teach you." His lips curved in a slow smile. "I want to be the one to complete your education, *señorita*," he added, slurring his words to underline the innuendo.

"You have Carmelita's education to take care of, so you needn't concern yourself with mine." Avoiding his eyes, she bent her head forward, rubbing the back of it where she had cracked it against the wall.

"Ha! So that's it!" A flash of laughter charged his

voice. "This tempest of yours is all because of what happened at the *fiesta*. You're angry because I left you last night to take Carmelita to Monterrey."

"Why should I be angry about that? As I recall, you pointed out quite clearly that I was not to involve myself in what you needed to do for Carmelita." Her words were as cold and brittle as an icicle.

"I assure you, I had no intention of upsetting you, and I certainly didn't mean to do anything that would make you leave; as a matter of fact, quite the contrary." There was a gentle apology in his tone. "You know I wanted to stay with you," he added huskily, placing his hand on her arm.

Shifting her position, she edged away, for his touch sent a wild flutter along her pulses. Ramon sent her a questioning look, then took his hand away. "I had no alternative, Gayle. Can't you understand that? I had to fly Carmelita to Monterrey right at that moment to make certain she would go." He rubbed his hand hard across his jaw. "She needed to be taken in hand. She's nothing but a rebellious child."

"I'd scarcely call her a child, Ramon. She's a beautiful, emotional girl."

"Emotional all right. And stubborn as a bull about Juan and that boat he wants. But we finally reached an agreement."

"What was the agreement?" She chewed at the corner of her lip, furious with herself because she was unable to hide her curiosity from him. "Or do you still suggest I stay out of it?" Her barbed words revealed her tension.

A muscle jerked in his cheek and his eyes were stormy. "You know, you can be as difficult to reason with as Carmelita." He rubbed his hand across his forehead, frowning with the effort he appeared to be making to keep a rein on his temper. "The terms were that she go to the university for at least one year, and in return, I shall arrange a loan for Juan, to enable him to buy this second boat he needs."

She uttered an exclamation of disbelief. "You're going to make it possible for him to have the boat he wants?" She slanted her eyes in speculation. "That *is* a payoff. Why, you're as sly and cunning as Dianne. Bribing Juan to force him to stay away from Carmelita." Keeping her eyes intently on his face, she shook her head slowly and gave a short, metallic laugh.

"What the devil are you implying?" His voice was loud and angry.

"I'm not implying anything. I'm saying right out that you and Dianne are a couple of clever schemers."

Leaning toward her, his eyes flashed with ire. "You're talking nonsense, and besides—what in blazes does Dianne have to do with any of this?"

"Just that, like you, she employs tricks to get what she wants, even if they don't always work. In her case, she used her father's magazine to try to get you away from Mexico. And *you* are using your money and influence to get Juan to give up Carmelita. Isn't that really what you want to accomplish?"

Taking her chin in his hand, he tilted her face and looked directly into her eyes. "I'm surprised at the venom that comes from such pretty lips." He traced the contours of her mouth with his finger. "Now I want you to keep them closed and listen to me." He put two fingers gently over her lips and held them there, as if to ensure her silence. "As to Dianne's

179

tricks, as you said yourself, they didn't work. I have no interest in her. As far as I'm concerned, she can stay in New York, where she belongs. I belong here, and with someone entirely different from Dianne Bennett." He tapped her lips softly, then, trailing his fingers along her chin, he moved a bit away and stopped touching her face.

She was sorry, and she missed the warmth of his hand the instant it was gone. It was as if she had been sitting in a shaft of sunlight and then a cloud had suddenly passed and blocked the warmth from her face.

"And though you seem to think I'm overbearing in forcing Carmelita to continue with her education," Ramon returned to the subject of the Mexican girl as if he had never veered away from it, "I have only her best interest in mind. I want her to realize all the things she should have, things that will bring her happiness."

Gayle ran her tongue across her lips. She felt as if the emotions churning inside her might erupt at any moment and betray her anguish to Ramon. "I—I understand all that you want for Carmelita," she said in a tight, strangled voice. Nervously, she swung her legs off the window seat, jumping to her feet. "It's getting late. The sun must have gone down; it's so dusky in here." She tossed the words into the air as she walked across the room. "I had better get down to the beach. Fernando will be coming to pick me up."

"Fernando's not coming. How do you think I got to the island?" He followed her, and putting his hands on her shoulders, he halted her progress toward the door. "I brought the launch and I'll take you back, but there's no hurry. I, for one, like the idea of being alone on this island with my amber witch." Her back was to him and his hands settled caressingly on her shoulders. As he spoke, his warm breath stirred her hair. Before she knew what was happening, he was kissing her neck in a way that caused a frightening weakness to flood through her.

Clenching her fists until her nails bit into her palms, she struggled to free her shoulders from his grasp. "I want to leave right now."

He tightened his hold. "Do you think I'm some foolish boy like Pablo, whom you can tease and inflame, then run away from?" His words hissed savagely against her ear. "Well, I'm not!" His voice was husky with the intensity of his feelings and he turned her around in his arms, forcing her to face him.

"Ramon, it was never like that. I didn't flirt with Pablo. You thought that, but it was never that way. You—you just imagined that it was. I—I never used you to prove anything, either." Her voice broke, and she found it difficult to force the words through her trembling lips. "I cared so much . . . I wanted . . ." She couldn't go on. Pulling back from him, she attempted to free herself. "I must go. I—I can't stay here with you."

"Can't? Or won't!" He held her, refusing to let her go. "Gayle, there's no understanding you." His eyes darkened with unmistakable desire. "Last night in the blending room, when you were in my arms, I'd have sworn that you didn't want to leave me. It was meant to be a special night for us, and if Carmelita hadn't caused such a ruckus, you know it would have been." His eyes held hers and his fingers moved first from her shoulders to the creamy whiteness of her throat and then up its length to cup her chin with a hand that had the touch of fire. "Nothing has changed. We are the same two people we were last night at the *fiesta*."

She closed her eyes, trying to shut out the image of his face so close to to hers, his lean, clean-shaven cheeks, and the passionate emotions revealed in his black eyes. "You're wrong. Everything has changed." She shook her head sadly. "Please, Ramon, let's not belabor this any further. I have made up my mind and I have to do what is best for me."

"Best for you? And what about what's best for me?" His lips were compressed in anger. "I at least have a right to know why you decided so suddenly to go back to the Napa Valley." He took her face between his hands, holding it firmly and forcing her to look directly at him. "You *will* explain why you're doing this. I won't let you leave this island until you do." All gentleness was gone from his touch and his voice. "You know, I think you would have left without a word if I hadn't come back from Monterrey today." His black eyes scrutinized her face. "You didn't want me to come back, did you?"

"No, I didn't!" Her voice rose; she was almost screaming. His hands hurt her cheeks and unbidden tears threatened to blind her. "I hoped I could be gone before you got back. I didn't want you to see what a romantic, silly fool I am, or know I'd been stupid enough to fall in love with a man who would never make a permanent committment to me." Hot tears stung her face as she flung the words at him with reckless abandon."

He stared at her in amazement. "What are you saying?"

Standing rigidly in front of him, she fought to hold on to some shred of composure. "You asked for an explanation and I'm giving it to you." She hesitated, clenching her hands to still her trembling fingers. "Last night, at the fiesta, I—I lost my head. When you showed me the label for your sherry, for one wonderful moment you made me believe you had named the wine Albariza Amber for me." She fought back a sob, drawing her breath in unevenly. "I almost believed that you cared and that I might just be the one blond American you'd be willing to accept in your Mexico." She closed her eyes, afraid to look at him. "Of course, I was mistaken," she said slowly, shaking her head.

"What makes you so certain you were mistaken?" His voice was husky, and he brushed his lips against her closed eyelids at the same time as he circled her trembling body with his strong arms and drew her close against him.

"Please—don't hold me like this," her voice shook. "Let me go."

"Not until you answer my question."

She knew she should draw away from him, but her body seemed unwilling to obey her mind. "I saw the portrait of your mother this morning. I asked Maria to explain why a beautiful painting by a fine artist wasn't hung on the wall at Casa del Mar."

An expressionless mask settled over Ramon's features. "What did Maria tell you?"

"About your mother's involvement with Valdez, all the time she spent away from you and your father." She managed to escape the intimate contact of his embrace. "Now I can understand why you have such strong feelings about American women."

183

"Does learning about my mother have something to do with your leaving?" He eased his arms, but kept his hands at each side of her waist.

"Yes, in a way it does."

"But why? You're nothing like my mother. You once told me that yourself."

"No, but I'm not like you either. I think you can find happiness only with someone of your own culture."

The lines at the corners of his mouth deepened. "Is the little would-be winemaker telling me she doesn't feel as I do about the growing of grapes and the blending of fine wine?"

"It's more than that," she said, trying vainly to keep her voice from shaking. He was now looking at her through lowered lashes in a strange, appraising manner that she found more unsettling than his touch had been.

"Didn't you tell me on the shell beach that day that you found my area of Mexico enchanting, and that you would be happy living in Casa del Mar forever because it was very beautiful?"

She could only nod her head.

"Then it seems you and I are not so different after all." He gave her a slow smile. "Besides, a few minutes ago you admitted being in love with me." His hands were warm and possessive and he stared down into her dazed blue eyes. "I know you love me, *querida*, because I could not love you so much if I didn't feel your love in return. I want you to marry me and stay at Casa del Mar always."

She felt his hand glide upward until it covered her breast. Her heart was racing and she felt the storm of her own clamoring emotions. She arched toward him as though he were a magnet pulling her close and she clung to him as he kissed her with an urgency that impelled a heated response from her lips. She was afraid—afraid of herself, and afraid of the sensations that were sweeping through her, sensations based on a need that she had never known before.

"No—No—" the words were a hoarse cry torn from her heart. She jerked away from him. "Ramon, Ramon," she repeated his name in anguish, "you don't love me; I'm not the one you really want." The words seemed to choke her as she pushed them from her dry throat. "You may not even realize it, but the reason you flew into such a rage with Carmelita last night was because you were jealous of her feelings for Juan. You love her, Ramon. You love Carmelita." The words tumbled from her mouth in a harsh frenzy of sound. "Don't you see, you've been nurturing her—educating her, because she's Mexican, and already, in so many ways, a part of everything here in your vineyards and in your way of life. She'll be the wife you choose." She turned and reached blindly for the doorknob. Her eyes burned with tears, and there was an agonizing tightness in her chest that felt as if it would stop her heart from beating.

In one swift movement, Ramon swept her up in his arms and carried her back across the room to the window seat. "*Querida—querida mia,* you are stubborn and foolish and beautiful." His arms were beneath her, cradling her against the warmth of his body. The way he was looking at her unleashed a storm of emotions within her. "What strange notions have filled that lovely amber head of yours." He touched her forehead with his lips. "You're right about one thing, however. I *have* taken it upon myself to nurture and educate Carmelita—but not for the reasons you've imagined." He gently put her down on the padded window seat and, staying close beside her, began to gently stroke her face, brushing away the dampness her tears had left. "Darling, Carmelita is my sister, my half-sister, that is. Esteban Valdez was her father. Maria and Fernando adopted her so my father would not learn that Mother had betrayed him."

Gayle's heart hammered in her breast and she stared at him, her eyes luminous. "I—I can't believe it!" She shook her head slowly, sighing incredulously. A barely perceptible smile began to tilt the corners of her mouth.

He cupped her face in his hands. "Now you can understand why Carmelita will, I'm quite certain, marry Juan, and with that determined stubbornness of hers, she will undoubtedly make sure he acquires a fleet of shrimp boats and equally as many children." He laughed and tilted her face up. "Not such a bad idea at that, is it?" She could feel the shaft of desire in his dark eyes as he looked into her face. Caressingly, his hand slid across her shoulder and down the length of her arm. He raised her hand and pressed his lips against her palm.

"*Querida mia*, it is this hand of yours which I wish to hold in mine for a lifetime." He pressed her hand between both of his.

She trembled inwardly at the look of love and longing in his eyes.

"I'm asking you to stay in my country, in my vineyard, in my *casa*, in every part of my life, Gayle, because we belong together." He lowered his face to hers. "Will you stay?"

Her lips parted in a smile of joyous awareness now

of the depth of Ramon's love for her. *"Sí, querido mio, sí."* She smiled up at him, saying the Spanish words he had taught her over and over until his arms closed tightly around her and his lips sealed off her voice. Then there was no further need of words, for she returned his kiss with all the love that rose from her overfull heart. That was the perfect answer for both of them.

Silhouette Romance

15-Day Free Trial Offer
6 Silhouette Romances

6 Silhouette Romances, free for 15 days! We'll send you 6 new Silhouette Romances to keep for 15 days, absolutely free! If you decide not to keep them, send them back to us. You pay nothing.

Free Home Delivery. But if you enjoy them as much as we think you will, keep them by paying the invoice enclosed with your free trial shipment. We'll pay all shipping and handling charges. You get the convenience of Home Delivery and we pay the postage and handling charge each month.

Don't miss a copy. The Silhouette Book Club is the way to make sure you'll be able to receive every new romance we publish before they're sold out. There is no minimum number of books to buy and you can cancel at any time.

This offer expires August 31, 1982

Silhouette Book Club, Dept. SBM 17B
120 Brighton Road, Clifton, NJ 07012

Please send me 6 Silhouette Romances to keep for 15 days, absolutely free. I understand I am not obligated to join the Silhouette Book Club unless I decide to keep them.

NAME_____

ADDRESS_____

CITY_____ STATE_____ ZIP_____

Silhouette Romance

IT'S YOUR OWN SPECIAL TIME

Contemporary romances for today's women.
Each month, six very special love stories will be yours
from SILHOUETTE. Look for them wherever books are sold
or order now from the coupon below.

$1.50 each

Hampson	☐ 1 ☐ 4 ☐ 16 ☐ 27 ☐ 28 ☐ 40 ☐ 52 ☐ 64 ☐ 94	Browning	☐ 12 ☐ 38 ☐ 53 ☐ 73 ☐ 93
Stanford	☐ 6 ☐ 25 ☐ 35 ☐ 46 ☐ 58 ☐ 88	Michaels	☐ 15 ☐ 32 ☐ 61 ☐ 87
		John	☐ 17 ☐ 34 ☐ 57 ☐ 85
Hastings	☐ 13 ☐ 26 ☐ 44 ☐ 67	Beckman	☐ 8 ☐ 37 ☐ 54 ☐ 72 ☐ 96
Vitek	☐ 33 ☐ 47 ☐ 66 ☐ 84		

$1.50 each

☐ 3 Powers	☐ 29 Wildman	☐ 56 Trent	☐ 79 Halldorson
☐ 5 Goforth	☐ 30 Dixon	☐ 59 Vernon	☐ 80 Stephens
☐ 7 Lewis	☐ 31 Halldorson	☐ 60 Hill	☐ 81 Roberts
☐ 9 Wilson	☐ 36 McKay	☐ 62 Hallston	☐ 82 Dailey
☐ 10 Caine	☐ 39 Sinclair	☐ 63 Brent	☐ 83 Hallston
☐ 11 Vernon	☐ 41 Owen	☐ 69 St. George	☐ 86 Adams
☐ 14 Oliver	☐ 42 Powers	☐ 70 Afton Bonds	☐ 89 James
☐ 19 Thornton	☐ 43 Robb	☐ 71 Ripy	☐ 90 Major
☐ 20 Fulford	☐ 45 Carroll	☐ 74 Trent	☐ 92 McKay
☐ 21 Richards	☐ 48 Wildman	☐ 75 Carroll	☐ 95 Wisdom
☐ 22 Stephens	☐ 49 Wisdom	☐ 76 Hardy	☐ 97 Clay
☐ 23 Edwards	☐ 50 Scott	☐ 77 Cork	☐ 98 St. George
☐ 24 Healy	☐ 55 Ladame	☐ 78 Oliver	☐ 99 Camp

$1.75 each

☐ 100 Stanford	☐ 105 Eden	☐ 110 Trent	☐ 115 John
☐ 101 Hardy	☐ 106 Dailey	☐ 111 South	☐ 116 Lindley
☐ 102 Hastings	☐ 107 Bright	☐ 112 Stanford	☐ 117 Scott
☐ 103 Cork	☐ 108 Hampson	☐ 113 Browning	☐ 118 Dailey
☐ 104 Vitek	☐ 109 Vernon	☐ 114 Michaels	☐ 119 Hampson

6 brand new Silhouette Special Editions yours for 15 days—Free!

For the reader who wants more...more story...more detail and description...more realism...and more romance...in paperback originals, 1/3 longer than our regular Silhouette Romances. Love lingers longer in new Silhouette Special Editions. Love weaves an intricate, provocative path in a third more pages than you have just enjoyed. It is love as you have always wanted it to be—and more —intriguingly depicted by your favorite Silhouette authors in the inimitable Silhouette style.

15-Day Free Trial Offer

We will send you 6 new Silhouette Special Editions to keep for 15 days absolutely free! If you decide not to keep them, send them back to us, you pay nothing. But if you enjoy them as much as we think you will, keep them and pay the invoice enclosed with your trial shipment. You will then automatically become a member of the Special Edition Book Club and receive 6 more romances every month. There is no minimum number of books to buy and you can cancel at any time.

Silhouette Romance

Coming next month from
Silhouette Romances

Song of the West by Nora Roberts

Samantha couldn't say good-bye to the windswept plains of Wyoming. Had she fallen in love with the countryside, or with the commanding rancher who had corralled her heart?

Stardust by Anne Hampson

Jody quickly fell in love with her business partner, Conor Blake, but seemed destined for heartbreak when her beautiful but cruel stepsister tried to steal his heart.

A New Dawn by Ellen Goforth

Cara Logan was determined to make decorating her career until she met Mathewson Daniels, an exacting client who demanded professional *and* personal attention.

Love Captive by Jacqueline Hope

Caught in a family feud, Anne McCullough was "kidnapped" by a furious Spanish gentleman. But after spending time with her handsome captor, Anne wished the feud would never end.

Nightstar by Fern Michaels

Chosen to represent Nightstar perfume, model Caren Ainsley was thrilled when New York's cosmetics king took an interest in her. Was he striving for success in sales or love?

Renegade Player by Dixie Browning

After escaping the stifling atmosphere of her father's wealth, Willemena reveled in her freedom. But her frivolous life-style might cost her the only man she'd ever loved.

Look for *Wildcatter's Woman* by Janet Dailey Available in May.